GETTING HOT

GETTING HOT

A Jail Bait Novel

MIA STORM

Getting Hot

This is a work of fiction.

Cover Design: Sarah Hansen, Okay Creations

Dedication

For everyone who reads.

CHAPTER 1

Bran

I shouldn't have fucked her last week. That was my mistake, and I feel like a douche—something I'm not used to.

I watch Destiny tuck a long strand of platinum hair behind her ear with her pen as she finishes taking drink orders at the table near the door. She shoots me a secret smile when she turns and makes her way over, and I mentally shoot myself for getting caught looking. This train's already careening down the track, barely holding onto the rails, and when I pull shit like this, it only picks up momentum.

"We got Hendricks?" she asks, slapping her order on the ancient mahogany bar between us.

I look over the order. "Closest thing I got is Tanqueray."

The smile falls off her face and she blows out a sigh. "I'll ask him."

I follow the curve where her tiny waist blooms into a killer ass as she turns and heads back to the table.

She's hot. That's what it boils down to. When I took her home last week, it was after her first training shift with Carol. We'd sat at the bar and knocked back a few after closing and I got caught up in everything she had going on. I totally missed the signs. I didn't see that she was looking for more than a hookup until after it was too late—until she didn't leave after we'd done the deed.

The only guy at the table with three women—some total wannabe with a dark suit jacket over a turtleneck and pressed jeans—scowls and gives Destiny some lip. I can't hear what he says over the piped-in Kat Country, but she shrugs and says something back, then offers me an apologetic squint when the guy pushes up from his seat. He starts my direction on polished loafers, but his eyes widen slightly and he pulls up short when he sees me.

The reaction's not unusual. When I left for boot camp eight years ago, I was already in decent shape. I was Oak Crest High's first ever (and only, as far as I know) four sport athlete all four years—football in the fall, wrestling in the winter, and baseball and track in the spring. Which is probably a big part of the reason my grades weren't good enough to do anything but enlist. But the Marines made all that training look like fucking Romper Room, and it was only a matter of weeks before my bulk didn't fit into any of my old clothes anymore. Since Pop owns the local gym and my sister Brenda runs it, when I'm not working behind Mom's bar at the Sam Hill Saloon, I spend most of my time lifting weights. I've managed to stay in pretty decent shape…which means guys like this pansy ass are generally intimidated. 'Course, the tattooed six-foot-three thing doesn't hurt the intimidation factor. Since I let my dark flattop grow out, I look more like a biker than an ex-Marine.

After a beat, his shiny shoes start moving again but he stops three feet short of the bar, out of my wingspan. "Tanqueray or Tanqueray Number Ten?" he demands, putting on a "big man" show for the women he's here with.

He flinches a little when I step aside to show him the rack behind me. "For top shelf gin, Tanqueray's what I got."

He closes his eyes for a moment and exhales his disappointment, then scans my top shelf again. "Tanqueray isn't even in the same league as Hendricks."

I shrug. "You want the citrus, I'd go with the Seagrams. Something drier, I've got Beefeaters."

He rolls his eyes toward the ceiling as if my suggestions are all so far below him he's afraid of getting a nosebleed if he has to look all the way down at them. "Just give me the Tanqueray. Make it a Tom Collins so I don't have to taste it."

He stalks back to his table and drops into his seat as I start on their order.

Destiny comes over and watches me mix. "That guy's a jerk," she says with a flick of her eyes back toward the wannabe professor. "Thank God he's Carol's to deal with in fifteen."

"You're giving Carol the tip?" I say with raised eyebrows.

Her lip curls. "Guys like that don't tip."

I lift my eyes to him as I shake his Tom Collins. "He give you a hard time?"

"He thought I should've known what kind of Tanqueray we have." Her face scrunches. "I didn't even know there were different kinds."

I glance at the table again. City folk for sure. Probably up here in the foothills for something at the college. "Guess he didn't realize he'd wandered out of his natural habitat."

She busts out a laugh as I pour his drink into the highball. "So, I was thinking…" she says when her laugh dies. "I could swing by your place when you get off. If you want."

"Listen…" I start, setting the drink on her tray. But just as I open my mouth to tell her I don't do relationships, Mom shoves through the swinging door from the kitchen. Six years in the Marines and two tours in Afghanistan, and I've yet to come across another single person who intimidates me…except my mom. She makes some of my Marine COs look like kindergarten teachers.

"Hey Vicky," Destiny says. "Has Carol punched in yet?" She tosses her eyes at Mr. Hendricks. "I'm giving her that table as soon as she does."

"She just clocked in," Mom answers, glancing suspiciously at the table. "What's the issue?"

Destiny shrugs a shoulder and picks up the tray of drinks I slide across the bar to her. "That guy needs to get over himself. Carol's better at dealing with people like that."

It's the "take no crap" chromosome in the Silo family gene pool. My cousin is almost as intimidating as Mom. She has a way of putting pricks like that in their place without them even realizing how it happened.

Just as I'm thinking it, I see her pass by the porthole in the wooden door to the kitchen, pulling her dark curls back into a ponytail. A second later, she pushes through the door.

She looks at the three of us and her eyes narrow as she slings her short, black apron under her bulging belly and ties it. "You guys do know that when everyone clams up and stares at you when you walk into a room, that's a dead giveaway they were talking about you, right?"

"All good, cuz," I say, lifting one hand in surrender while picking up my bar rag with the other.

She gives us a glare that could fry bacon. "I'm not fat."

"No, you're not," Destiny says, handing her the tray of drinks. "But I'm punching out and I need you to take that table."

Carol's gaze shifts to the table in question. "What's wrong with them?"

"The guy's a sanctimonious prick," I say wiping down the bar. "He needs to be reminded his shit still stinks in the way only you can."

A slow smile tugs at her mouth and she takes the drink tray.

"He's the Tom Collins," Destiny says. "The chardonnay is for the girl on his right and the Cosmos are for the other two."

She bats her eyelashes and starts toward the table. "Coming right up," she says, all breathy and sweet.

Mom turns to me once she's gone, her frown deepening. "I came out here to remind you to put a note in the drawer if you pull petty cash, Bran."

I give her a dubious smirk. "Really, Ma? I've been doing this for almost a year. Think I've got the drill down by now."

"Well, the drawer came up exactly sixty short last night. So how else do you explain that?"

I feel my brows lift. My drawer's never off by anything more than a few pennies. "You sure you didn't pull it for the wine order?"

She scowls at me and crow's feet crease the corners of her eyes. "I might be old, but I'm not senile yet."

For her age, I have to say Mom looks pretty damn amazing. She met Dad sometime in the stone ages, when she used to dance at a strip club in San Francisco, and even still, I can see why he picked her out of the crowd.

She's got a deep worry line at the inside corner of her right eyebrow, but otherwise her face is deceptively youthful. The only thing that gives her age away is the skunk stripe that starts on the left side of her forehead and winds through the sea of dark hair pinned onto the back of her head like the first swirl of cream into black coffee.

"I didn't take any cash, Ma. Seriously."

She sighs wearily and rubs her eyes. "It's been a long day. I'll check the numbers again tomorrow morning when I can think."

I lean down and give her a peck on the cheek. "'Night, Ma."

She hooks her elbow around my neck and yanks me in for a hug. "See you tomorrow, baby boy."

She's the only one I'd ever let call me baby or honey or any shit like that because, like I said, I'm a little scared of her. I watch her disappear through the kitchen door.

And then it's just Destiny, waiting for an answer.

I take a deep breath and blow it out slowly as I turn to her. "Listen, Destiny. There's no question you are fucking amazing, and I had an awesome time the other night...but I feel like you might have gotten the wrong idea about what this is." I drop the bar rag and splay my hands on the bar between us, holding her gaze. I may be a dick, but I've got a moral compass that points in the right general direction most of the time. She deserves to be told straight up. "I'm not the kind of guy that does relationships, and even if I were, you wouldn't want one with me."

It's not like I expect her to whine or beg. I've only known her for a week, since Mom hired her for day shifts, but she seems generally more together than that.

What I also don't expect is a shameless smile to spread over her face as she leans closer. "So, are you saying that pounding me until I see stars is too much of a commitment?"

I blow out a laugh and give my head a slow shake. "This isn't how I pictured this conversation going."

She pushes away from the bar and unties her apron. "I'll be back before closing. Maybe have a drink or two. And when you leave, if you take me with you, you won't be sorry. If not…" She shrugs. "…no harm, no foul."

I watch as she disappears through the kitchen door to punch out. Carol drops another drink order on the bar on her way to the kitchen and I go back to work.

The Friday evening crowd picks up and it's not long before all the tables are full and patrons start lining the bar. I dim the lights—the closest we come to ambiance.

The Sam Hill Saloon has been here since the gold rush, when the town of Oak Crest was established as a mining camp. After they got married, Dad brought Mom out here and bought her this bar to keep her "busy," since he didn't want her taking off her clothes for horny men anymore. She got it in the divorce and has run it for the last thirty years, but the truth is, almost nothing here has changed for nearly three quarters of a century. There are pictures on the walls of grimy gold miners lined up at this very bar. Even most of the chunky wooden barstools and tables have survived. At some point, some owner lined the front wall under the windows with three booths, and Mom added a big-screen TV and sound system, but other than that, it looks exactly like the pictures. And there's the faint stench of stale beer emanating from the floor planking that no amount of bleach will ever get out.

But it's a landmark, and the only bar in town, so we're usually busy.

I'm blending a pair of frozen daiquiris with one hand and shaking a martini with the other when out of the corner of my eye, I see a solo blonde slide onto the barstool at the end, near the beer taps. I finish what I'm doing and prepare the tray for Carol to pick up before glancing over and seeing it's Destiny.

A guy in the middle of the bar makes eye contact and nods at his empty beer mug. I grab it and start filling without really looking up at her. "Didn't think I'd see you again till closer to closing."

"Sorry?" she says. "Are you talking to me?"

The voice is off—slightly raspy and a pitch lower than her usual. I look up again and squint at her, wondering if she's already started drinking. She's taken her straight hair down from the ponytail she always wears it in and it's not as long as I remember it from the other night—the only other time I've seen it down. There's also a fading blue stripe cutting through the platinum over her right ear that I've never noticed before.

"What can I get you?" I ask her instead of pushing it.

I'm already reaching for the vodka and cranberry to start on a Madras, her drink of choice last week, when she answers, "Rum and Coke."

"That's different," I mutter, shooting her another glance.

She gives me a puzzled look. "Look, I really just wanted to find out if you hire entertainment."

My face mirrors her puzzlement, I'm sure, as I try to process her statement. "Why?"

She hunches to the side and pulls something up from next to her feet. I see it's a battered black guitar case when the narrow end peeks over the top of the bar. "Because I need a gig."

"Didn't know you played," I say, pushing her drink across the bar to her.

That baffled look is back as she pulls it toward her and takes a swallow. I can't help following the curve of her long neck downward toward a pair of large round tits perfectly outlined by her snug, low-cut T-shirt. She is definitely hot, and if we're on the same page, then I've got nothing to feel guilty about. She wants me to fuck her till she screams? I'm perfectly capable of that. She sets her drink down and catches me staring. She cuts me that wicked smile again, causing my cock to stir. I return the smile, sending the innuendo right back at her.

She props her elbows onto the bar and leans forward, giving me a clear look down her shirt. "Considering that we've never met before, I don't find that surprising."

I'm so absorbed in images of my face buried in those magnificent tits that it takes me a second to process what she said.

My eyes snap to hers. "Wait…what?"

She reaches across the bar, offering me a hand. "Lilah Morgan."

There's a full second all I can do is stare, wondering if this is one of those split personality things you hear about sometimes. And in that second, through the dim lighting, I take in all the tiny details—a dark mole at the outer corner of her right eye; her eyes, silver instead of blue; the missing white crescent-shaped scar above Destiny's right eyebrow; and lips, a little fuller than I remember—which are smirking at me now.

"You're not Destiny," I say as it all clicks.

It's not a question, but she shakes her head. "No. I am most definitely not Destiny."

"Twins?" I ask.

She cocks her head playfully. "What do you think?"

"You've got to be. You're fucking identical except for the eyes." I tap my forehead. "And you're missing a scar."

Her perfect blond eyebrow rises in amusement. "She's the pretty one and I'm the smart one."

I bark out a laugh as I reach across and shake her hand. "Bran Silo. Good to meet you."

She doesn't let go of my hand for a second after we're done shaking—just long enough to send a clear message that she's interested.

A knot forms in my gut when I realize I've got a situation. Destiny and I have an understanding, but regardless, I'm pretty sure fucking her sister would be way outside the bounds of gentlemanly behavior. Not that anyone would ever mistake me for a gentleman. "Destiny never mentioned she had a sister."

"Doesn't surprise me." She takes another drink, nearly polishing it off in a few big gulps.

I tip my head at it her glass. "Another?"

"My limit is one," she says, pushing her glass toward me. "Just Coke this time, thanks."

Carol sweeps by on her way to the kitchen, dropping an order on my bar. "Thought you left," she says to Lilah without slowing down. "Careful or your favorite customer might ask for you," she adds, jerking her head at Mr. Hendricks as she disappears through the swinging door.

I laugh as I scoop ice into Lilah's glass and fill it with Coke. "Good to know I'm not the only one."

Lilah shrugs. "Happens all the time." She slides out of her chair, lifting the guitar case. "So do you want to hear me play or what?"

I look around the crowded room, loud with chatter, drowning out the background music. "We don't generally have live entertainment," I say, which is really an understatement. We've *never* had live entertainment. But for some reason, I'm not willing to shut Lilah down so fast.

When my eyes find her again, annoyed impatience shines loud and clear out of her gaze. "So that's a no?"

I feel my mouth pull into a cocky half-smile. "I didn't say that."

She opens her case and pulls out her guitar, unabashedly climbing through the window I left ajar for her. I watch as she sets herself up on the stool and rests the guitar in her lap, gripping it softly but confidently. She starts strumming, and I expect her to be discrete, since this is basically an audition, but there's not a shred of self-consciousness or embarrassment anywhere in her disposition as she begins to belt out lyrics—an old No Doubt song that I can't remember the name of.

The way she plays, as if on instinct, the passion in her voice, and the fact that she's really fucking good, starts to turn heads at the tables closest to us. As they quiet and listen, more tables still, and soon the only thing she's competing to be heard over is the Kat Country on the speakers. But she doesn't decrease her volume. If anything, as eyes find her, she becomes louder, feeding off the attention.

I reach under the bar and click off the stereo, then lean onto the back counter and cross my arms, listening as she finishes one song and launches into the next.

A guy at the bar pulls a five from his pocket and flags me down with it. I grab his beer mug, but he shakes his head. "Is there a tip jar?" he asks with a nod toward Lilah.

I pull a fresh mug from under the bar. He slips the five inside and I set it at the end of the bar near Lilah. She cuts me a smile and her eyes slide down my body as she sings.

And *fuck me*. I lean my hands on the bar and press against the lower counter when my dick won't yield to my will. Without a doubt, everything Destiny has going on, Lilah's got that and more.

CHAPTER 2

Lilah

Destiny's mentioned Bran occasionally since she started working at Sam Hill last week, but she never mentioned how brooding, unapproachable, and totally ominous he is—over six feet of pure testosterone, packaged in ripped muscles and a solid frame. His face is all hard lines and dark stubble. And nearly black eyes smolder like hunks of burning coal under the thickest lashes I've ever seen. Based on the five o'clock shadow and the ghosts roughening his features, he's got to be mid-twenties. Which is old enough that my body shouldn't be reacting this way. But that knowledge doesn't stop my blood from boiling with every scorching glance he gives me across the bar.

And he's giving me a lot of them. Long, shameless perusals of my body as I play. I'm on my eighth song and he hasn't told me to stop yet. He even put a tip jar out and people are shoving bills into it.

So I keep smiling and playing.

I never really got how our parents ended up together. Dad is way older than Mom and used to be fat, before he started tweaking, with a round face, long nose, watery gray eyes, and male-pattern balding that started in his twenties, based on the pictures I've seen. After I saw that Barbie *Rapunzel* movie when I was four, I was totally convinced that Mom was really Rapunzel and had gotten lost from her kingdom. The gene pool was kind to Destiny and me and we've got Mom's coloring and kickass body—the only thing either of us really has going for us.

So I put it on display for the hot bartender.

I spread my legs as I readjust on the stool between songs, and a shudder ripples through me when Bran's simmering gaze follows the rise of my skirt hem.

There's been a few times in the past I've had to use my body to get what I needed. A little flirting and flaunting goes a long way. But no one's ever made me *hope* it would come to that before. Let's just say, if I have to flirt my way into this gig, it won't break my heart.

I debate whether to do some of my original music, but my best friend Shiloh and I found out in the BART and bus stations we used to play, before Destiny dragged me out here to the sticks, that people tip better when they know the songs. I sum up my audience and pick songs from their teen years—early 2000s for this group. Remind them of their glory days and tips double.

So I launch into some Mariah.

I'm not a great singer, but I can hold my own. We used to make bank in San Francisco because of Shiloh. We called ourselves LohLah and had dreams of making it big someday. She's one of those rare people that you just know is going to be a star. Her voice is so hot it could melt steel and so pure it could shatter glass. But lots of people have great voices. Lo has more—looks, attitude, and a magnetic presence that demands your attention.

She tried to talk me into going with her when she auditioned for *The Voice* this summer, but I don't have what she does. From the start, I knew she was going to make it. She was chosen for the blind auditions in L.A., and one line into her song, all four coaches' chairs turned. She chose Adam as her coach. I watched her cut like butter through the battle rounds, and her last iTunes release rocketed up to number two, behind Taylor Swift's new single. She made it into the top twenty last week and the judges are using words like "totally original" and "the real deal" to describe her.

But Lo was more than just my bankroll. She was the only thing that kept my head from imploding when everything went down with my parents. She was my rock.

God, I miss her.

Five hours later, as the bar starts clearing out, I've emptied the tip jar into my guitar case three times and it's overflowing again. When he's not pouring beer or mixing drinks, Bran's gaze has been searing me alive from the far corner of the bar. He stands there with his arms crossed over his massive chest, biceps straining the sleeves of his T-shirt, reminding me of a panther crouched in the grass, ready to spring.

"You did okay," he says, nodding to my tip jar.

"Looks that way." I gather the bills and loose change from my case and stack it all on the bar. There has to be at least a hundred dollars.

He pushes away from the counter and stalks over to me. "I can't pay you, so you'll probably only want to come in Friday and Saturday nights when we're full."

The heat of his scrutiny causes a trickle of sweat to roll between my breasts and tighten my nipples. "I'll be back tomorrow," I say, tucking my guitar safely away in its cradle, trying to decide if I want him to notice or not.

"Seven to closing?"

I shrug, knowing I can't stay until closing, but also wanting to get here after Destiny leaves at six. "Something like that."

"You're good," he says, pulling a pair of tens from his tip jar and shoving them into mine.

I grab the jar and add the cash to the stack. "I know."

Out of the corner of my eye I see him smirk. "And modest."

I glower at him. "Explain to me how modesty is going to the pay bills."

He holds a hand up and his smile changes from a smirk to something more suggestive. "Point taken."

I really want to follow the suggestion in that smile to see where it leads, but it's nearly midnight and Destiny's going to start flipping out if I'm not home soon. My midnight curfew is my own fault, so I really can't give Destiny too much shit. She got a lot dumped on her when our parents blew up the kitchen, burnt our house to the ground, and ended up in jail for cooking meth. Overnight, she went from avoiding home altogether to essentially becoming a parent.

But it was the day she found out I was tweaking that her over-protectiveness kicked into high gear. Maybe she hopes she can bring me back from the brink. Who knows? Whatever it is, I know her heart's in the right place, and she's done okay keeping things together, so I try not to disappoint her too much.

I cross Main Street and walk under the streetlights to the end of the block. The gun and ammo shop is dark inside and the barred security door is locked. But to the left of it is a rickety wooden door that a stiff breeze would probably blow over. I turn the lock and the hinges creak loudly in the midnight quiet as I pull it open. I lock it behind me and climb the steep, narrow staircase to the door at the top, knowing I'm fifteen minutes late and knowing Destiny will be waiting up, expecting an explanation. I push the door open and find her in the kitchen.

"Where have you been, Delilah?" It's out of her mouth, all maternal concern, before I'm even fully in the door.

"I think I might have gotten a job." I scratch my head with my free hand. "Sort of."

Her eyes widen. "Doing?"

I tuck my guitar case into the corner near the door and pull the cash out of my pocket, setting it on the table. "Playing on weekends at the bar you work at."

"That's where you were?" she asks, her eyes lifting from the cash to mine, searching for the lie.

"All night," I reassure her. "Ask Bran."

Her expression turns sour. "I don't like the idea of you hanging out in a bar."

Of course she doesn't. We came here to get me clear of tweakers. Not that I saw anyone who fits that bill at Sam Hill. "It's not like there are any BART stations here. It's the only place I could think of to play."

When we needed money for the PG&E bill or whatever, Lo and I would go play the subway stations. It's impossible to find a job in the city if you're not at least eighteen, but we did well enough with our music that I could cover most of the utility bills. Even though it's cheaper to live in Oak Crest, Destiny only has one job. Resignation slides over her face as she thinks about our situation and comes to the same conclusion I have.

We need the money.

"You're sure you're ready?" she asks with a questioning squint.

"I'm fine now, Destiny. Seriously." She's right to ask, because only a week ago I wasn't. But I'm over it now.

"They're good people there," she says with a weary sigh, then scrutinizes me for another few seconds before adding, "As long as it's only weekends."

"Bran says that's probably the only time I'll make any tips, so…"

The concern on her face is replaced with determination. "Then I'm going over to Oak Crest High on Monday to enroll you. If you're ready to play at Sam Hill, you're ready to go back to school."

I look down at the stack of cash. The thought of starting a new school in the middle of October makes me throw up in my mouth a little. "I was thinking about getting my GED instead."

"Uh-uh," she says. When I lift my eyes to hers, she's shaking her head and scowling. "Mom and Dad already stole your childhood. I'm not letting them take high school from you too."

I just look at her. "Shouldn't that be my choice?"

"No."

Her dismissal pisses me off. I might have screwed up, but I'm not a baby. "There's nothing I'm going to get out of high school, Destiny. This isn't like the city. I can get a regular job here…help with the bills and whatever. We won't always be broke."

She shakes her head again. "First of all, I think you have to be at least eighteen to get your GED, and second, it's not just high school, Lilah. It's your whole future. You're going to college."

An incredulous laugh erupts out of me. "Really? Because if I remember right, *you* didn't go to college."

Chagrin clouds her face. The bank had foreclosed on our house in Lower Haight way before my parents burned it down, but because there was a kid living there— me— the bank was having trouble evicting us. We all had things we guarded with our lives. Destiny's was the fact she had a job at McDonald's and she'd used that money to buy her crappy green Dodge Neon, which she didn't tell our parents about and never parked near the house. Mom's was the coffee maker on the counter. Mine was my guitar and my doorknob. Metal had started to go missing around the house—things like cabinet pulls and door handles. Since our parents stopped paying anything a few years before they blew up the house, the only reason we had electricity was because Destiny made payments on the bill. And appliances mysteriously started to go missing. The washer and dryer were the first to go, followed a few months later by a gaping hole in the kitchen when the dishwasher disappeared. The refrigerator survived, as well as the stove, probably because Dad needed it for his new line of work.

For the last few years, it was sort of an open door policy—all my parents' tweakbuddies crashing on our floor or whatever. Our house always had squatters, and they got so creepy I started keeping a carving knife under my bed. My parents never cooked anything but meth, so they didn't miss it. Destiny got caught up in that life more than me, I guess because she was older. She barely graduated high school from what I remember.

"I know first and last months' rent cleaned us out when we moved here." I nod at the money. "I just want to help."

She takes a deep breath and steps out from behind the counter. She's dressed to slay, in fuck-me heels and her shortest, tightest little black dress. "Listen, Li. I'm working on something that will fix everything. I'm going out tonight. Might not be home until morning."

There are nights that Destiny doesn't come home, but she's never brought a guy back to our apartment. I think she's trying to shelter me, even though she knows I'm no virgin.

Which she discovered at the same time she discovered I was using. Overall, not my best moment.

Tyrell was our apartment manager's son. We met when I had to walk the rent down to their apartment five months ago because it was already late. He invited me in and we hung out, played some Minecraft, smoked some weed. He was six-five and blacker than night, which I remember thinking was pretty hot. To this day, I still don't really know how old his was, but I'm guessing maybe nineteen or twenty.

Long story short, I started hanging out there every day after school and it's the classic story of one thing leading to another. Over a few months, pot led to crack and making out led to sex.

I don't blame Tyrell. I don't think we were really in love or anything, but he's mostly a decent guy. Just a little misguided. I let my like of him fuck with my guidance system too. My mistake.

But, whatever.

Anyway, the pieces started to click—though I've never asked her quite which pieces and how—and one day about three weeks ago, Destiny, who was supposed to be at work, was instead pounding on Tyrell's door. She dragged me, half-naked, out of there, screaming at Tyrell that I was only sixteen and she was calling the cops. She didn't, but three days later we were in a U-Haul on our way to Oak Crest.

And she hasn't looked at me the same since.

She inhales and grabs her bag off the other kitchen chair at our tiny table. "Lock up after me. I've got my key."

I follow her to the door and she gives me a hug before passing through. When she's gone, I go to the table and drop into a chair. I pull the stack of money toward me and start counting. Including Bran's twenty, there's a hundred sixty nine dollars and thirteen cents. Not bad for five hours of solo work.

Who would have thought Podunk would be so profitable?

Destiny's best friend from high school went to Sierra State and moved in with her boyfriend not too far from here after she graduated in May. She told Destiny it was cheap and she should come. So here we are.

And she was right.

Our apartment in San Francisco was in the Tenderloin, the scariest part of the city. It was a studio, so Destiny and I both slept on a pull-out couch. Here, we each have our own bedroom, and the great room with the kitchen and living room is bigger than our entire apartment in the city. It may be nearly as run down as our old place, with water stains on the ceiling and appliances that are older than my parents, but so far I haven't seen any roaches.

This is a much safer town, but old habits die hard. I take the money with me to my room and stuff it into my pillowcase. I get ready for bed, but once I'm in with the lights out, I find I'm anything but tired.

I never really sleep. Nightmares will do that—screw with your head when your defenses are down. I doze, but then images of flames tickle the edges of my awareness and pull me from the arms of slumber. And just before I snap my eyes open, there's always blood. Destiny's, I think, from the cut on her head.

But tonight, I know I'm not going to get that far. I feel like I drank a thousand cups of coffee, every nerve ending still buzzing from the last five hours of Bran Silo's eyes scorching over my skin. But it's more than that. His physical form is impressive, but his presence is immense. And raw. And totally invasive, winding its way into my synapses and taking up residence there, leaving me so fucking wired I feel like I could crawl up the wall and stick to the ceiling like Spiderman.

This feeling is way more addictive than booze or any drug I've ever tried. But addictions are dangerous. Addiction robs people of control, steals their free will. People do stupid things for addiction—fuck up their lives, give up their futures. I've seen the end result of addiction up close and personal, and it's not pretty.

Never let it be said that my parents didn't teach me anything.

And now I know how slippery that slope is. I thought I was stronger than Mom and Dad. I thought I was in control when I was using. But our first two weeks here were hell and there are two full days I lost completely with the withdrawal. I never would have made it through without Destiny.

"Stay the fuck out of my head, Silo," I tell the ceiling.

Because, unlike my parents, I learn from my mistakes.

CHAPTER 3

Bran

I lay with my fingers laced behind my head, staring at the whirring ceiling fan. I haven't even moved to pull the condom off my flaccid dick because I wanted Destiny to fall asleep. Judging by the twitching and the little squeaking noises she's making, I finally got my wish.

Painstakingly, I peel each of her fingers off my chest, then lift her arm slowly before carefully extricating my legs from hers. Sort of like diffusing a landmine. One false move and *kapow!* When I'm free, I slowly sit on the edge of the bed and peel the condom off. I go to the bathroom and clean up, then tug on some boxers. On the way to the living room, I scoop my phone off the dresser.

I'll never admit to my ex-roommate Marcus that I miss his sorry ass, but since he couch jumped to his sister's place in Oakland to be closer to his girlfriend, this place is too quiet. If he were still sleeping on my couch,

I'd grab a couple of brews from the fridge, crack him over the head with one to wake him up, then we'd sit and stare at whatever stupid Chevy Chase flick was playing on late night TV until sunrise.

What can I say? It's a guy thing.

But he's not here, so instead, I start the coffeemaker perking, then move to the dark window and stare up at the stars.

What the fuck I am doing?

I've fucked dozens of girls. Hell, probably hundreds. The college just up the hill supplies a steady stream of fresh pussy. Maybe it makes me a dick, but I don't even know most of their names. As long as we're all in it for a good time, I've never come away feeling wrong about it. But from the minute Destiny showed up at the bar before closing tonight, I've felt this prickly, itchy feeling, like ants under my skin. And the whole time I was on top of her, all I could picture was her fucking sister.

Or really, *fucking her sister*, if I'm honest.

I've known Lilah for thirty seconds and she's totally under my skin. No one's *ever* gotten under my skin.

When the coffeemaker starts sputtering, I go to the kitchen and pour a deep mug, then drop onto the couch. I down half the cup in one long swallow, shove my earbuds in, and flip my phone to the clips I recorded earlier at the bar. Lilah playing some pop song. But it doesn't sound pop the way she does it. It sounds...unique. Better.

It's not the kind of thing I usually listen to. My playlists are full of pounding bass and angry rhythms. Disturbed's *Indestructible* was my anthem during both tours in Afghanistan. I'd be out sweeping for mines and it would be cycling through my head on repeat. It kept me sane. Kept me focused. Kept me from thinking about how many guys with my job end up going home in body bags...how many of my friends had already gone home that way.

Which is the real reason for all the girls since I've been back. Sleep is dangerous. Defenses drop. You're vulnerable to attack.

And not just from the outside.

Because it's those internal demons that will destroy you if you let your guard down for even a second. They're much more lethal than anything in the outside world.

Which explains why I haven't actually slept in six years. If I can keep the adrenaline going, I can stay at least partly awake, and fucking some poor girl senseless is my preferred mode of nocturnal adrenaline delivery.

But it's getting old. Which means the rush is mostly gone. Each new face just runs into the river of old ones and it all becomes a meaningless blur. Nothing new. Nothing exciting. At this point, it's more habit than therapy anymore.

I shake my head at myself and blow out a disgusted laugh. How pathetically predictable am I? I'm a walking cliché.

I loll my head back and start on the Gettysburg Address. If I knew it this well in high school, I probably wouldn't have barely squeaked through U.S. history. As boring as it might sound, trying to get through the entire thing without making a mistake keeps my mind from going anywhere darker. But Mr. Lincoln can't keep my interest tonight, because on my phone is the sexiest fucking voice I've ever heard, like smoke over gravel, rough with a purr on the kick, singing about the hell she's going to rain down on her man.

Which makes me wonder if she has a man. Truth is, I've been wondering that all night. She left early, before midnight, like someone might be waiting for her or she had somewhere to be. It's not like I could bring it up while I was fucking Destiny. "Hey, so what's the deal with your twin sister? She seeing anyone?" But fuck, I feel myself bristle at the image of Lilah riding some lucky shit who's not me.

That girl tugs at me on so many different levels, my stirring cock being the most evident. I fish it out of my boxer briefs. The rasp of her voice wraps around me as I stroke and I'm instantly hard. I close my eyes as her voice invades me, makes me vibrate to her frequency. I tense, my whole body sinking into the fantasy, and growl as I feel a hard rush tighten my balls. And when I come like a rocket all over my stomach and chest a few minutes later, I hiss "Fuck!" between my teeth.

I am a fucking douchebag. Destiny's in the other room, in my bed, and in my mind, I'm fucking her sister on the couch.

I had the whole convo again last night with Destiny before I brought her home. She says she's on board with no strings. But something about the way she clings when I climb off her makes me think she's only saying that because she knows it's what I want to hear.

I grab a dirty T-shirt from the floor and clean myself up, then go for another mug of coffee. Several hours and at least a hundred repeat Lilah clips later, the room pinks with a new day. About the time I'm deciding to drag my ass off the couch and brew a second pot of coffee, Destiny comes out of my room, poured back into the tiny black dress she showed up to the bar in last night.

"Hey," she says when she sees me. "You couldn't sleep?"

Telling her I never sleep will only lead to more questions, and it's not like I can tell her the specific reason for my insomnia tonight, so I just shrug as I pull myself up from the couch. "Woke up early."

She drops her heels to the floor with a clatter and climbs into one shoe. "Everything okay?"

As okay as ever. "Sure. Want some coffee?"

"Sorry..." She glances toward the door. "I need to go. But I'll see you later at work."

"Yeah, right." I should probably move to see her out, but I don't.

"So...thanks for last night." She offers a smile with all kinds of innuendo buried in it as she slips on her other shoe. "It was great."

"Sure." Fuck, I hate this awkward shit. Which is why I vowed after the last time I did this not to fuck anyone from work anymore. Because shit like this is inevitable. "See ya later."

Once she's gone, I go to the kitchen, brew a new pot, and bring it back to the couch with me. I should just mainline the shit. I refill my mug and take an enormous gulp of the scalding liquid, then lift my phone and replay the Lilah clips again, trying to find in the sound the drug that has me so fucking addicted already.

Destiny is on days, getting her bearings so she can make the jump to nights fulltime when Carol goes on leave for the baby in a few months, which means our shifts only overlap by an hour. Mom comes in at nine to do all the admin, then takes the bar from opening at eleven to when I show up at five. Destiny usually clocks out somewhere around six.

I told Lilah to come in at seven. For some reason, I really don't want Destiny here when she arrives. Not because I don't want Destiny to know I'm into her sister. At the gym this morning, I decided I need to be up front with Destiny and tell her what we got going on just isn't working for me. More, it's just fucking awkward.

Because the other thing that became glaringly apparent when I couldn't shake her sister out of my head, no matter how hard I worked out, is that unless Armageddon comes, I don't think I'm going to be able to stop myself from fucking Lilah eventually.

Mom is at the bar when I clock in and I wipe everything down while she finishes up the tray for Destiny's only table—a group of college guys in the corner. Mom likes to think of Sam Hill as a restaurant that has a bar, but the state of California has decreed we are a bar that serves food. What that means is our servers are technically cocktail waitresses and have to be twenty-one. And as much as Mom disagrees, it's really true. The kitchen doesn't even open until five. We get a few tables every night looking for dinner, but Jim, our cook, is mostly busy putting together plates of nachos or chicken wings for drunk Sierra State students when they get the munchies at ten. It'll be another few hours until things really start to pick up.

Mom hands the tray off to Destiny, who smiles at me and then turns for the table. I watch as the five guys eye her appreciatively. She is totally scorching, which probably makes me the stupidest fucking moron on the planet, but I've always gone after exactly what I want and her sister is no exception. I might be a douche, but even a douche has limits. I'm not going to fuck them both at the same time.

Unless they want me to.

The thought causes my dick to stir.

"Your drawer was another forty short last night, champ," Mom says, pulling my attention back to her. "You gonna tell me what's going on?"

I will my cock into submission and turn to face her. "You sure it wasn't that way when I took it over?"

She tugs the bar towel off her shoulder and chucks it at me, then starts through the door into the kitchen. "I'm never off."

"Neither am I!" I call after her, but the door swings shut before I finish.

When I spin to draw myself a beer from the tap, Destiny's sliding the tray onto the bar. "I'm sore," she whispers. "You really worked me over last night."

"About that..." I top off my beer and set it down between us. "Don't take this wrong. You're fucking incredible in the sack. Really. But I'm just not feeling it."

Before the whole thing's out of my mouth, she's already shaking her head. "Is it because I stayed? I won't next time. You just wore me out."

She's not the first to say that. I don't hold back and I guess I'm too much for some girls to handle.

"That's part of it, but I'm also feeling like you might be looking for more than just a fuckbuddy. I need to be right up front and tell you I'm not looking for anything exclusive."

She spins the tray on the bar. "I told you, I'm not looking for anything serious, Bran. If you want to see other people, be my guest."

I search her face and she seems sincere. "You seriously wouldn't have a problem if I took someone else home?"

She shakes her head and a devious smile tugs at her mouth as she glances at her table of guys. "Would you?"

"No, doll." I blow out a laugh. "Knock yourself out."

She twitches over to the table and makes the rounds, asking if they need anything else and striking up a conversation with a blond guy with his back to me. I can't hear them over the music, but there's no mistaking the body language. She's selling and he's definitely buying.

Carol pushes through from the kitchen, tying on her apron. "I don't think I'm going to make it two more months," she says, glaring at her enormous belly. "I'm so much bigger this time."

"Suck it up. You're fine. Wanna beer?"

She shifts her glare on me. "You know I would kill for a beer." She shoves back through the kitchen door leaving a muttered "bastard" in her wake.

Destiny clocks out at five and when she passes back through the bar on her way out, the guy she was flirting with gets up. One of his buddies knuckle bumps him. She glances over her shoulder at me and waves on their way out the door.

So I guess she wasn't joking. She's not looking for exclusivity. But I still think fucking her sister would be crossing a line.

The bar gradually fills and when Lilah comes in just before eight, there's hardly an empty seat in the place. I only realize how tense I was, wondering if she was going to show, when I feel my shoulders drop a few inches at the sight of her.

And she is a fucking sight to behold.

Her long blond hair is twisted onto the back of her head and when she pulls off her hoodie, she's in a tight tank top and a shorter skirt than last night. The contours of those perfect tits, tiny waist, and round ass kick my heart rate up a notch.

The row of guys who were at the bar last night are back and applaud when she comes through the door. The table with the drunks Destiny was hanging out with catch on and they start wooting, like they think she's going to stand on the bar and strip for them. Lilah grins and blows kisses with a flourish, not at all embarrassed by the attention.

She makes her way over to the empty barstool at end of the bar. "You saved me a seat."

"You bet your sweet ass I did. My tips nearly doubled last night, and all these assholes are back because of you," I say with nudge of my chin at the three guys seated on the stools next to her. "In the bar business, asses in seats is a good thing."

Especially her incredible ass. The fantasy of it parked on my face flashes in my mind and the rush to my groin hardens my cock.

I top off the beer I'm pouring and set it on Carol's tray, then lean my elbows on the bar across from Lilah. "You should think about sticking around after closing tonight."

Her eyes flick up at me and they comb over my pecs as she unpacks her guitar. "Oh, yeah? Why's that?"

I shrug. "Thought we could have a beer, get to know each other. Whatever."

She smirks. "And what exactly does 'whatever' entail?"

"Just about anything you're up for." And I just left that line I wasn't going to cross in the dust. What the fuck am I doing?

I shove off the bar when a guy in the middle flags me down. When I'm done with his drink, Lilah's already started playing.

I set her tip jar up on the end of the bar, then lean into the far corner to watch her. I wasn't imagining it. That voice is pure sex.

"Got any requests?" she purrs when she wraps up her first song.

I bark out a laugh.

She tips her head and raises her eyebrows, challenging me.

I stalk closer and brace my hands on the bar across from her. "You wouldn't know anything I'm into."

"Try me."

"Slipknot," I say, confident that she'll ask me if that's a song or a band.

Instead, she gives me a cocky half smile and starts strumming the opening chords to "The Devil in I."

It's different, but good. She puts her own spin on it and, even though it's the same song I've listened to a thousand times, it sounds totally fresh.

And fuck me if I don't want her even more.

I know I told myself fucking Destiny's sister was crossing a line, but the longer I watch her the more I hope "whatever" turns into my tongue on every inch of her body before my cock sinks balls deep inside her. It's been a long time since I was this turned on by a woman. I know for fucking sure that this is one face that isn't going to blend into the river. I'm going to fuck her raw and remember every second of it.

CHAPTER 4

Lilah

It's nearly eleven thirty and the way Bran's been looking at me for the last three hours, as if choosing which part of me to devour first, makes me ache in places I've never ached before.

No one has ever looked at me like that. Not even Tyrell. When we fucked, it was because we were stoned and horny and bored. But I'd bet everything in my tip jar that what Bran has in mind for me has nothing to do with being bored. That look is pure animal lust mixed with a healthy shot of testosterone. His hormones are speaking and mine are most definitely answering.

Hell, the way my nipples tighten every time he looks at me, my hormones may as well be yodeling off a mountaintop.

The crowd tonight is younger on average than they were last night, so my playlist has been more current. I've thrown in my best metalhead selections for Bran's benefit. I strum the last chord of KoЯn's "Hater" before reaching for the rum and Coke I've been nursing all night.

I should probably tell him that I'm not legal…for anything…but I like that he thinks of me as mature instead of the little girl that Destiny treats me like. After everything we've been through, you'd think she'd see that I can hold my own…that I don't need to be protected. After all, it was me who noticed the fire first. You'd think that would count for something. But all she can see is me following in Mom and Dad's footsteps. She won't give me any credit for learning from my mistakes. Just the fact that I'm perfectly fine stopping at one drink is all the proof I need that I'm not them.

I finish the drink and set the glass down. Bran is fucking me with his eyes as he refills it with ice and Coke and my nipples bead against my shirt again. I don't think there's much doubt my body wants to follow through on that eye-fuck. He thrills me and intimidates me all at the same time and something about that combination makes me hornier than I've ever been.

His biceps ripple as he pushes off the bar, but he doesn't back away. He stands there devouring me with his eyes. I want so badly to take him up on his offer and stay after closing, but if I'm not home on time, Destiny will come looking for me. If she finds me with Bran, we'll be in another U-Haul tomorrow, on our way to another nowhere town.

At least this town has Bran.

So, instead, I slip off the stool and put my guitar away, then empty my tip jar into my bag. "I need to head out."

Bran leans his hands on the bar across from me, his pecs flexing with the motion. "Why?"

"Someone's waiting for me."

His full red lips press into a line and he nods slowly. "You'll be back next weekend?"

"If you want me."

His eyes flash an inferno into mine. "I definitely want you."

I gush into my panties as my breathing goes shaky. I take a deep breath to settle my nerves. "Then I'll be here."

I feel his eyes follow me to the door and when I pass through, the cool night air feels good on my scorched skin. I take my time walking home and feel the fire inside me begin to cool. I hope by the time I walk through the apartment door three minutes before curfew that my face isn't still flaming.

Destiny's on the couch with a tub of chocolate ice cream, watching one of the Jurassic Park movies. "How did it go?"

I pull the money from my bag and lay it on the table. "Probably around a hundred."

"They're too polite around here not to tip good."

"Looks that way," I say, sliding into the chair. I start sorting and count. One hundred and forty six tonight.

"Grab a spoon," she says when I stand, unfolding her long legs from under her and sitting up straighter.

I go to the drawer and grab one, then drop onto the couch next to Destiny.

She hooks her elbow around my neck and pulls me closer. "I think we're going to be okay here."

The raised crescent scar on her forehead rubs against mine and the image of blood floods my memory. I can barely remember a time when Dad didn't hit Mom, but other than yelling at us any time we happened to cross his path, he mostly ignored Destiny and me. But that scar has something to do with Dad—and the fire. I just can't remember what, exactly. Destiny and I don't talk about that night. Ever. So, instead of asking any of the myriad questions that have haunted me for the last two years, I dip my spoon into the ice cream. "The waitressing is working out?"

"The money's not great yet, but it will be better when I take over nights in a month or two. And I've got a longer-term plan in the works. I'm feeling pretty good about things, actually. You?"

I nod as I lick my spoon. "It's way different from home. I miss Lo. But I think it will be good. Like I said, I can get a real job here and—"

"I thought we agreed you're starting school next week," she cuts in, all concerned mother.

I grab a handful of hair. "Why?"

"Because you're sixteen, Delilah! It's the law. We don't need the local authorities deciding you're truant and snooping into our business."

I blow out a sigh. "Fine. But I'm still getting a job. I'll find something after school."

She nods, relieved. "As long as you still have time to study. School first."

"Fine," I repeat, even though the idea is about as appealing as vomit on toast.

"Have you met Vicky?" she asks me, settling deeper into the cushions and pulling her legs back up now that it's settled.

"Who's Vicky?"

"Bran's mom. She owns the bar, but she's probably gone by the time you get there."

"Must be. I haven't met her."

"And Bran?" she asks.

I can tell she's still looking at me and I keep my eyes on the TV, because at Bran's name, I'm suddenly hot all over. "What about him?"

"He's sort of intimidating, but he's a really great guy."

"He seems okay," I say, working to keep my tone indifferent.

She gouges out a huge hunk of ice cream. "Hoping he's also the jealous type."

Something in my chest turns to stone and my eyes snap to hers. "Why?"

"Because I walked out tonight with another guy, so if he's not, that long-term plan I'm working on may very well backfire."

I can hardly breathe. "Bran is your long-term plan?"

She sets the ice cream down and turns her body to face me. "We need stability, Lilah. Bran's family has run that bar forever. They make good money."

I'm suddenly ice. "Do you love him?"

She huffs a laugh through her nose and shakes her head. "I've only known him for a week."

"So…I'm not following."

"I think it could become something, is all I'm saying."

I can't even think. "I'm going to bed," I say, standing. I take my spoon to the kitchen and get ready for bed, but my heart is pounding so loudly in my ears that there's no way I can sleep.

But what I know is, I can't go back to Sam Hill next weekend.

Or ever.

CHAPTER 5

Bran

It's Friday and I'm wound so fucking tight that I can't stand still, because I haven't seen Lilah anywhere but in my fantasies for the last six days. And those fantasies have been mind-blowing.

When she left last Saturday, she said someone was waiting for her, which probably means she's got a boyfriend. That would be an obstacle, but not one I'm too worried about. I've seen the way she flushes when she looks at me, the way her nipples prick to tight pebbles under her shirt—the same way my cock responds to her.

So, there's one thing I'm certain of: I am going to have Lilah.

The *when* is less certain.

I'm pacing behind the bar, trying to sort in my head how long I need to wait before I can fuck Destiny's sister without being an asshole. At first, I thought a month, but now I've convinced myself maybe a week is good enough.

Because my undeniable truth is that she's consumed my mind. I haven't been able to think about anything else all week long. Every night, I've stretched out on my bed, pressed my earbuds in and listened to her sultry voice until the sun came up. I'm convinced if sex could sing, it would sound just like Lilah.

Eight comes and goes, but I don't start flipping my shit until after nine when she's still not here. I get so far as to go into the office and pull up Destiny's file on Mom's laptop to find her number. I could call her, but then what? Even with my moral compass spinning out of control, I know that asking Destiny why her sister didn't show up for an unpaid gig is a little off.

It's almost nine-thirty and I'm still watching the door like a hawk when Carol leans on the end of the bar and rubs her swollen belly. "I don't know what I was thinking when I thought I wanted another kid. I've changed my mind."

I tear my eyes away from the door and look at her. "A little late for that, do you think?"

She scowls. "Everything is so much worse this time. My feet are swollen, I can't eat anything without heartburn, I have to pee all the time, and I can't sleep. And if I survive all this, my reward is a screaming baby to go with my ornery one-year-old."

"I thought you said Wyatt always gets the second nine months," I say, shoving away from the bar and drawing another Bud for the guy on the stool next to the one I've saved for Lilah.

"I'm hauling it around for the first nine," she says, heading for the kitchen, "so you damn well better believe it!"

I set his beer in front of him and realize he's watching the door almost as intently as me.

"Dude, what happened to the entertainment?" he asks, gesturing with a nudge of his head at the empty stool.

My stomach tightens. "Damned if I know."

I snap the towel off my shoulder and start wiping down the bar for the thousandth time tonight. My eyes track back to the door when it opens and I hold my breath. When my sister Brenda comes through with a guy I don't recognize, I crack a smile. Not who I was hoping for, but the next best thing.

I give the patrons at the bar a quick glance to be sure they're set, then head to the booth in the corner, where the guy ushers Brenda. There's no way I'm not checking this guy out. The last guy she dated, this fucktard Nate, didn't understand the word "no" and Brenda had to fight him off one night. Now he's in jail on multiple counts of rape. It started when my ex-roommate's sister, Blaire, came forward with something that happened way before Brenda. But once Blaire made the accusation, the dominoes started falling and seven other women, including Brenda, ended up testifying at his trial.

I sidle up to the table as they get settled and size the guy up. He's blond, blue-eyed, and older than me by a few years, maybe pushing thirty. But he's in decent shape and looks like he spends a fair amount of time in the sun, based on his tan.

I squeeze my sister's shoulder. "Everything good at the gym?"

She scowls at me, knowing exactly why I'm here. "It hasn't burnt down since you were there six hours ago."

"I'm Bran," I say, holding out my hand to the guy and giving my arms and chest their best flex. "Brenda's older brother."

"Trevor," he says, pumping my hand. "Good to meet you."

He's got a faint southern twang. Nothing that would knock you over, but noticeable.

I nod. "Haven't seen you around here."

"Just took a position up at Sierra State this fall," he says, letting go of my hand, "so I'm new to the area."

"What position?" I push.

"I'll have a Blue Moon," Brenda says, kicking me under the table. When I turn my gaze on her, she's lighting me up with a glare that could cut steel.

"It's okay, Brenda. He's just looking out for you," Trevor says, and instantly, he gains a few rungs on the ladder. "I'm the new head groundskeeper, so none of that fancy academic stuff. Don't have the brains for that."

I slide into the booth next to Brenda and she elbows me. I can still feel the heat of her glower. "What's your accent? Sounds southern."

"Alabama born and bred."

"So how'd you end up here?"

He shrugs. "Got divorced at the beginning of the year. It was kind of complicated and made staying in our hometown hard, so I decided if I had to move, may as well make it count."

I think about asking why the divorce, but I'm not getting a "domestic violence" vibe from this guy so I let it drop.

"Okay, then." I stand and give my hands a clap. "What can I get you to drink?"

Trevor waits for Brenda to order her beer, and as he's asking for a Seagram's and Seven, the door opens again.

My heart hiccups when it's who I've been waiting for all night.

The stripe in Lilah's hair is purple tonight, and when she shucks off her hoodie, she's in a tight pink tank top with a black bra underneath and a short black skirt. Miles of toned, tanned legs stretch down to a pair of short black boots.

I want to map every inch of those legs with my tongue.

Her eyes lock on mine and I'm suddenly electrocuted. My synapses overload and I stop dead in my tracks and just stare.

"Hey," she says.

I force myself to breathe and start my feet moving. We walk to the bar together without looking at each other.

"Thought you weren't coming," I say as I round the corner and start on Brenda's drinks.

I'm not totally successful keeping the frustrated undercurrent out of my voice, and I know she hears it when her eyes narrow as she sets her guitar on the stool.

"I wasn't."

"Why?"

She goes back to unpacking her guitar. "Why didn't you tell me you were dating my sister?"

"Because I'm not."

Her eyes snap to mine. "That's not what she says."

I shake my head. "We hooked up a couple times, but we both agreed we're not looking for anything exclusive."

Her lips pucker and those silver eyes harden to steel. It looks like she's got more to say on the subject, but instead, she lowers her guitar case to the floor and slips onto the stool. She looks right at me, holding my gaze as she starts to strum. And when she launches into Carrie Underwood's "Before He Cheats," all my guts turn to lead.

So, it looks like a week is probably optimistic.

Carol comes by and I give her Brenda's order, then mix Lilah's rum and Coke and set it in front of her with a tip jar. She blasts through three more songs about dirtbag guys before she stops and chugs her drink.

"So, if you weren't coming, what are you doing here?" I ask, refilling her glass with straight Coke.

"I need the money." She messes with the tuning knobs at the end of her guitar and strums a few times.

"What did you do before you moved here?"

"Nothing but this," she says with a wiggle of her guitar. "Me and a friend made bank in the BART stations." She pulls her guitar into position, but her gaze stays on me. "What about you? Have you always tended bar?"

"Got out of the Marines two years ago."

I watch her silver eyes flit over my arms and I feel them as if she was brushing her fingers over my tattooed skin. When they find mine again there's something in them I can't read. "How long were you in the Marines?"

"Six years."

"Six years," she repeats, her eyes widening.

"Two tours in Afghanistan."

She nods slowly as her gaze combs over my face. "Glad you made it home safely."

I blow out a laugh. "Me too."

"Do you miss it?"

But before I can answer, the guy on the stool next to hers, who I'm now realizing I should have cut off two beers ago, starts unbuttoning his shirt and says, "Army. Got this in Iraq."

He pulls open his shirt to reveal a scar on his stomach, and behind him, his two buddies elbow each other and stifle a laugh.

I look the guy over. There's no way he's older than me. Probably younger. "Where were you stationed?"

"Baghdad," he says, still showing us his beer gut.

"Which camp?"

His eyes pull away from Lilah and he squints as he tries to focus his beer goggles on me. "Why do you care?"

"Because Army forces pulled out of Iraq in 2011. I don't see how you're old enough to have been there before that."

His blurry eyes widen and then track back to Lilah as he stumbles off his stool. "He's a fucking liar." He lurches toward her as his buddies snicker under their breath.

I leap over the bar and pin him against it. "Don't you lay a fucking hand on her."

I grab him by the back of the neck and escort him to the door as he hurls a string of protests my direction. He resists when I haul him outside and pin him against the wall with a forearm across his throat.

"There's nothing I hate more than lowlife posers. Good men died over there so you can jerk off in your own fucking bed every night. You stay the fuck out of my bar or next time you'll leave bloody."

His buddies stumble through the door just as I shove him out of my grasp and one of them grabs him by the arm to keep him from toppling. "C'mon, Mike."

He grumbles something that I don't bother to listen to as I slam back through the door.

Lilah is mid-song when I come back in and she gives me a look as I step around her to the tap to draw myself a beer. When she finishes, she says, "He was my best tipper."

"He was dick," I say, grabbing a fistful of green from my tip jar and shoving it into hers.

Carol slaps a drink order on the bar and I get to work on it. When I'm finished, I look up and my already boiling blood heats for a whole different reason with the way Lilah's gaze rakes over my chest and abs. When it pauses at my belt buckle and she licks her lower lip, my cock predictably responds. So maybe a week isn't out of the question after all.

She plays and I listen, feeling every fantasy I've had about her taking root in my dick. My T-shirt is a little too snug and short to hide the growing bulge in my jeans, so I don't even try. I want her and I want her to know. No clearer way to demonstrate the point than to give my hard-on free rein.

A couple comes in and takes the stools Poser and his buddies where occupying. I set them up with a Greyhound and a Midori Sour. When I glance at Lilah, her eyes lift from my package to my eyes and there's an unmistakable spark in them. She noticed. She shifts in her seat and her voice roughens even more on the refrain of "Take Your Time." Don't know who sings it, but it's all over the radio the last few months. And the message in the song and all over her face tightens my cock even more.

I refill my beer and let the cocky smile spread. I take a quick sweep of the bar, clearing off a place that a guy has vacated and shoving his tip in Lilah's jar.

"That was yours," she says when she finishes her song.

I arch an eyebrow at her. "What? I'm not allowed to tip you?"

"You did already," she says, fishing the bills out and sliding them across the bar to me.

"That was for Poser." I shove the money back at her. "This is for me."

She looks at me for a few long heartbeats before taking it.

"Another rum and Coke?" I ask, holding up her empty highball.

She contemplates that for a second before saying, "Sure, but light on the rum."

I mix her drink and set it down in front of her as she starts on her next set. Brenda's man settles up with Carol and they come over to say bye on their way out. Little by little, the bar clears out.

Lilah starts packing up at around eleven thirty and my heart skids to a stop.

I lean on the bar and fix her in my gaze. "Stay till closing."

For a long second, she just stares into my eyes and I feel the crackle of electricity at the connection. But then she shakes her head. "Can't."

I take a deep breath as she heads up the hall to the bathrooms and brace my hands on the bar to keep from following. I know it's out of line, but I want just one minute alone with her.

Just as I push off the bar to follow, a girl from the middle booth up front pushes out of her seat and staggers toward the bar on four-inch fuck-me red heels.

She leans on the bar, her substantial rack all up in my face. "Fuck me from behind," she purrs.

I follow Lilah with my eyes until she disappears into the ladies' room, then give the redhead in front of me a quick once over. Just my type—killer bod and no name.

I picture her pressed up against the wall out back, her tiny skirt around her waist. My balls pull tight at the image of pounding her, fucking all this frustration out of my system. But in my mind, she morphs into a tall blonde with an hourglass figure and a purple stripe in her hair.

Nothing but the real deal is going to satisfy this hunger.

CHAPTER 6

Lilah

When I come out of the bathroom and head back to the bar, there's a redhead with dark roots leaning across the bar toward Bran, her huge boobs ready to tumble out of her low-cut shirt.

I'm back at my seat in a flash on a wave of jealousy-charged adrenaline…just in time to hear her say, "If you don't have the coconut, you can make me a Wet Pussy instead."

He braces his hands on the bar and his jaw tightens as he glances sideways at me. "I've got the coconut."

I turn my back and pack away my guitar, trying to shake the sense that my jealousy is personal. This is about Destiny. She likes him. He's slept with her. He shouldn't be ogling some other bitch's tits. I shoot a quick glance at him as the redhead slides onto an empty barstool and tells him a Fuck Me From Behind is shaken, and not to be gentle, and I realize he's really not ogling her. He looks mostly indifferent.

Until his eyes shift to me as he strains the drink into a shot glass. The cold disinterest turns to molten heat and those black eyes flare.

Destiny made good on her threat to register me for school and I started Wednesday, so my days are swallowed up in a blur of useless information. I went to the park with my guitar after school yesterday and found a bench near the play structure at the top of the hill, hoping the moms and dads there with their screaming kids might find the music soothing and tip well. I made twelve dollars in two hours. So I had no choice but to break my vow to stay clear of Bran. I'd convinced myself that I could be in his presence and not be affected. I'd told myself he's just a player, like half the guys in my high school, only with more experience—that he looked at every other woman in the bar the same way he looked at me.

I was wrong.

The heat in his gaze has nearly scorched me every time his eyes scour my body. I feel like I've spent the last three hours in a sauna. When he looks at the redhead, there's no fire in his eyes. Not even a simmer.

So what does that mean? And the bigger question: how does he look at Destiny?

I don't really want to be anywhere near Bran when Destiny's there. I know how my body reacts to his presence and there's no way I could hide it from my sister. They've slept together. Now that I know that, I thought I'd see Bran in a new light. I thought that would stop the flood of hormones he seems to unleash in me.

Not so much.

I shouldn't have come back, but until I can find an actual job, I need the money.

He sets the drink on a bar napkin and pushes it across to the redhead. She sips it and her red lips pull into a lascivious smile. "Perfect."

I yank my bag off the bar and head for the door.

"Lilah!" Bran calls from behind me. When I turn, he's rounding the end of the bar, moving toward me. He stops just in front of me and it feels like I'm caught in a solar flare. "You'll be here tomorrow?"

"Unless I get a better offer," I say, flicking a glance at the redhead, who's watching us with dagger eyes.

He nods slowly. "Just checking."

I spin for the door, because the redhead at the bar might have gotten the drink, but I'm the one getting wet. And that can't happen. "I'll tell Destiny you say hi."

When I hit the sidewalk, I take a second to catch the breath Bran stole from me, then try to clear my head.

It's still spinning when a voice comes from behind me. "Hey."

I turn, expecting Bran, but instead see the guy Bran threw out. His friends are nowhere to be seen.

"Hi."

"You're probably thinking I'm some kinda stalker," he says, his words fuzzy with alcohol.

I hug my guitar case in front of me like a shield. "The thought crossed my mind."

He holds up his hands. "I just wanted to apologize."

"For...?"

He takes a step toward me. "I was a dick in there. It's my birthday and the guys were buying me drinks. I guess I had a few too many."

"Happy birthday," I say without moving.

He laughs. "Would have been better if I coulda not gotten my ass booted outa there."

"So, was he right? Were you lying about the Army?"

His smile turns sheepish. "Yeah."

"So, what's the real story?"

"Where you headed?" he asks, instead of answering.

"Home."

"I'll walk with you and tell you the whole sad story."

Does this guy seriously think he's coming home with me?

"You know what?" I say, my hand rifling through my bag. "I left my keys on the bar."

"I'll wait," he says as I back toward the door.

The redhead is still at the bar and one boob, partially encased in a black lace bra, has fully escaped her shirt now. Bran is leaning toward her on his elbows and she's laughing shamelessly at something he said. He smiles...until he sees me standing in the door.

Carol's passing by with a tray of drinks and stops. "Hey, hon. Everything okay?"

"Yeah. Just waiting out the creep Bran threw out of here earlier."

Her eyes widen. "What do you mean, waiting out?"

"He's out there," I say with a jerk of my thumb at the door.

"Seriously," she says, glaring at the door. "Want me to call the cops?"

"I think that's probably overkill. He'll get the message when I don't come back out."

"Normally I'd do this myself, but..." She rubs her belly. "Hey, Bran!"

I glance his direction and see he's at the end of the bar wiping the counter, but he's watching us.

"Stalker," Carol says, with a tip of her head at the door.

Bran steps around the bar. "Can you keep an eye on things in here?" he asks Carol.

"Got it," she says heading with the drinks to the group in the corner.

He grasps my elbow and I'm totally unprepared for the electric rush as he pulls me aside. "What's going on?"

"That guy you threw out was waiting for me outside."

His eyes narrow and cut to the door. "Fucking dick," he says under his breath.

"I just figured I'd wait him out," I say with a shrug.

"Like hell."

He slams through the door and I follow.

Stalker is standing with his hands in his pockets, grinning. But the second he sees Bran, the grin falls off his face.

"I thought I told you if you showed your face here again, I'd bloody it," Bran snarls.

He lifts his hands in surrender and staggers back a step. "You said not to set foot in your bar, dude. I didn't."

Bran takes a step. "But you're stalking my friends, which isn't cool with me."

The guy glares at Bran. "You know, you're a fucking piece of work. You go off and blow up a bunch of people because George fucking Bush told you they're terrorists, and now you think own the world."

"Go home," Bran says, rage oozing out with the words and turning them into something darker. "I'm not having this conversation."

"Figures you'd say that," Stalker spits. "Because then you'd have to think about all the babies you killed."

Bran is in his face the next second, pinning him against the wall with a forearm to the windpipe. "Get the fuck out of here. I'm not going to say it again."

He shoves away from the guy, who grabs at his throat and staggers back.

"Fascist," he snarls, then turns and lumbers up the sidewalk.

"C'mon," Bran says to me. "I'll walk you home."

Neither of us moves for a minute and I realize he's waiting for me to show him the way. I'm honestly not sure if I'm any more comfortable with Bran walking me home than the stalker. "You're still on the clock. I'll be fine."

He shakes his head, staring into the darkness in the direction Stalker just went. "No way I'm leaving you alone out here with that pervert."

I start toward the middle of town. He keeps step at my side.

"Did you?" I ask.

He glances sideways at me. "What?"

"Kill babies."

His jaw grinds tight and there are several footsteps where we're silent. "I don't think so," he finally says, "but you never really know sometimes. Things happen fast, or the intel says a building is clear, and then you find out it's not." He shrugs. "You can let that shit eat you alive, or you can tell yourself you did the best you could and move on."

I stop on the corner to wait for the only traffic signal in this shitty town to tell me it's safe to cross, even though there's not a car in sight, and turn to look at him. "Which have you done?"

He looks at me for several beats of my speeding heart, then steps into the street without waiting for the light. "You see that guy anywhere near you, I want you to call me." He pulls his phone from his pocket. "What's your number?"

I rattle it off with a shake in my voice and he types it into his phone. The next second, mine is ringing.

"Save that number in your contacts," he says. "Better yet, speed dial. You even think you catch a glimpse of him, I want to hear about it."

"I don't think he's really dangerous."

His feet slow as he looks at me all protective. "Nothing is beyond a guy who'll do something like that to get a girl to hook up with him."

"Okay," I say, typing SOS into the name spot on contacts. I don't want Destiny to see his number and think I have a reason to want it.

We reach the gun shop and our door just beyond. "Thanks," I say, digging in my bag for the key.

He looks around, his brow creasing. "This is it?"

"Home sweet home," I say, unlocking the door.

He still looks unsure as the door creaks open. "This isn't the greatest area."

"But it's the cheapest."

"My complex is pretty cheap," he says.

I step through and turn to face him. "Three seventy-five cheap?"

He shakes his head then looks over the door lock. "The landlord should replace this entire door and frame. There's dry rot. Anyone could just kick this in."

I shrug. "You get what you pay for."

He scowls at the deadbolt a moment longer then swings the door most of the way closed. "Lock up."

I flick him a sharp salute. "Yes, sir."

He raises an eyebrow and those dark eyes drill through me. I think he's going to yell at me about disrespecting the uniform or something. Instead, he says, "And don't forget it," then closes the door. I twist the deadbolt and a second later, the knob rattles and the door shakes. "Tell him to replace this door," he calls through it.

"Yes, sir," I repeat.

"Good night, Lilah," he says, then I hear the fall of heavy boots on the sidewalk.

I press my hand against the door, listen until his footfalls fade out, and climb the stairs to the apartment.

Destiny's in the kitchen, mounding spoonfuls of chocolate chip cookie dough onto a baking sheet.

"My birthday's not until January," I say, dumping my tips on the table.

"They say the way to a man's heart is through his stomach."

Bran. My stomach cramps as I drop into the seat and start sorting bills.

She turns and nods at the money. "How'd you do?"

I think about telling her what happened with the stalker, and that Bran walked me home, but decide she'll only panic and tell me I can't go back. "I got there a little late, so not as good as last weekend."

She rinses her hands and brings a plate of cookies to the table, slipping into the chair across from me. "Still looks like a pretty decent haul."

"I guess so." I watch my hands stack the cash into a single pile. "A redhead was hitting on Bran when I was leaving the bar."

She sighs heavily and reaches for a cookie. "Doesn't surprise me."

"You're not jealous?" I ask, lifting my eyes to her now that I think my face won't betray my own jealousy.

She nibbles at the edges, obviously uncomfortable with the thought. "We're in the 'I'm giving him space' phase of our relationship."

"What does that even mean?" I ask, grabbing a cookie off the plate.

"It means Bran thinks he doesn't do relationships, so if I push him, he's going to push back. But I can see the truth in his eyes. The string of women is getting old. Before too much longer, he's going to realize he wants more, and I'm going to be the one who gives it to him."

"Seems like an awful lot of work," I mutter, my mouth full of gooey chocolate. Despite the fact I think I was four the last time our mother baked cookies, and she stopped cooking altogether by the time I was ten, Destiny's got the baking thing down. While Grandma was teaching me guitar, she taught Destiny everything she knew about pastries and cookies and cakes. Everything she makes is amazing. But we usually don't have the money. "You really think Bran's worth that kind of effort?"

"I have responsibilities." She threads her finger through the hair on the top of her head and grabs a fistful. "I need someone who's steady and reliable and can support us."

I nearly choke on my last bite of chocolaty goodness and feel my eyes widen as I realize exactly what she meant by "long-term plan." "You want to *marry* him?"

"We need this, Lilah."

I force myself to swallow. "But why Bran? I mean, you're gorgeous. There have to be a million guys who would want to marry you who aren't player bartenders."

"Because I like him," she says with a self-conscious shrug. "He's exactly the kind of guy I want. He's strong and loyal and…" Her face scrunches in embarrassment. "He's crazy hot, Li. Once he comes around, he'll be amazing."

"Crazy hot" is an epic understatement, but I don't correct her. What I say instead is, "You've known him two weeks, Destiny. He could be an ax murderer for all you know."

She shakes her head. "I've seen how he treats the people he works with. He's a really good guy, Li."

"Carol's his cousin, right? And pregnant. He's going to treat her good."

"He even treats the cook, Jeff, like family. And you should see him with his mom. He turns into a big teddy bear. I'm telling you, he's one of the good ones, even though he doesn't seem to realize it yet."

"If you say so." I blow out a breath as I stand and head up the hall. "Good night."

She pushes up from her chair. "'Night, Li."

I take the money with me and tuck it into my pillowcase. When I finally turn out the lights and get in bed, I realize I'm shaking a little. I guess Stalker freaked me out more than I realized.

Or maybe it's just the things Branson Silo does to me—and the things he makes me want to do to him—that scares the crap out of me.

CHAPTER 7

Bran

I'm under the hood of my car, still sweating from my morning workout at the gym, when Destiny pulls up in her green Dodge Neon.

Dread snakes through my gut as I gear up to explain, once again, that I'm not into her.

She pulls into an open space across from my carport and I stand and lean against the fender. She's in shorts and a tight T-shirt, which showcase all her best assets. And in her hand is a big baggie of chocolate chip cookies.

"I haven't seen your car in the daylight," she says, and it occurs to me, as much as they're nearly identical on the outside, Destiny's voice doesn't pull at my balls the way Lilah's does. "It's awesome."

I wipe my hands on my jeans and pat the hood. "She's my baby."

There's an awkward silence and she holds out the bag. "I made some cookies last night, but if I eat them all they'll go straight to my ass, so…"

I take them. "Thanks."

"So…" she says, fidgeting with the strap of her bag. "I was just on my way to the bar, but I wanted to stop by with those."

"Then I guess I'll see you later," I say, setting the bag in the V between the open hood and the windshield.

She just stands there as if waiting for me to say more, but I'm not sure what she's expecting. Finally, she opens her mouth.

"If you don't have other plans, I could stop by with some ice cream after you get off tonight." She nods toward the cookies. "Those make killer ice cream sandwiches."

I take a deep breath. "Listen, thanks for the cookies. Seriously. But, I meant it when I said I just don't see this happening again," I say with a wave of my hand between us.

She tips her head. "I'm only talking ice cream sandwiches, not diamond rings, Bran."

I shove a hand into my hair and blow out a long breath. May as well come as clean as I can at the moment. "You are totally hot, and I had an amazing time with you, but there's someone else I'm sort of into right now."

Her eyes widen slightly before she can fully contain her surprise. "The redhead at the bar last night? Lilah told me about her."

At her sister's name, my insides prickle with a rush of adrenaline. "It doesn't matter who, Destiny. I told you before I'm not really feeling this, and that hasn't changed."

Her mouth presses into a tight "oh well" half smile and her eyebrows go up as she backs away a step. "Just thought we were having fun. If you're not into it anymore, no problem."

I lift the bag. "You want these back?"

She looks over her shoulder at me as she turns for her car. "Of course not. I made them for you."

And with that slip, I know for sure nothing about this is casual for her. I totally fucked up bringing her home.

"Thanks," I say, reaching into the bag and popping a cookie into my mouth.

She gives me one of those flirty finger waves as she lowers herself into her car. "See you tonight."

As she drives away, I think about Googling a way to delay labor, because one hour of shift overlap is going to be awkward enough. I don't even want to imagine what being at the bar all night every night with Destiny's going to look like once Carol's gone.

Especially weekends when her sister is sitting on my barstool ear-fucking me with that smoke-over-gravel voice of hers and making me hard as stone for her.

I jacked off again last night thinking about her on top of me, riding my hard cock. I haven't done that since high school. Even on base, there were plenty of opportunities. But now every opportunity pales in comparison to the one who's holding out on me.

I'm fucking obsessed. That's the only word that describes the grip Lilah has on me. And tonight, if I get the chance to be alone with her, there's no fucking way I'm not going to grab it.

I call Mom and tell her I'm going to be a few minutes late, then drive the long way past Lilah's apartment. I roll up to the curb and get as far as cutting the engine before I realize just showing up here makes me as bad as that asshole stalker from last night. I flip my phone from my pocket and look at her number. The only other women in my contacts are Ma and Brenda. I don't get hookups' numbers. Hell, I usually don't even know their names. But I needed Lilah's. Her ringtone is one of the clips I taped of her. My finger hovers over the call button for a really long time before I hit it.

"Hello?" Her voice is cautious and I'm sure she's wondering why the fuck I'm calling her.

So am I.

"Hey. It's Bran. Just wanted to check if you needed me to pick you up tonight." Yeah...totally lame.

"Why would I need you to pick me up tonight?" she asks, skeptical and still wary.

"Because that pervert might still be hanging around."
I don't mention that *this* pervert is parked right outside
her apartment. "Carol could cover the bar if I swung by
for you around seven."

"No, thanks," she says. "I can get there on my own."

"You walked last night," I say, thinking out loud. "Do
you have a car?"

There's a pause. "No."

"Then I'll be walking you home again tonight. I don't
want you out there alone in the dark."

The line goes dead and I realize she hung up on me.
Dark rage climbs out of the deepest pit of my soul, where
I keep it caged, and I fling my door open. But I'm not
even out of the car before better judgment wrestles with
the rage and wins, sending it back into the pit. Breaking
her door down is not going to accomplish anything but
demonstrating exactly why I'm wrong for her—why I'm
wrong for *anyone*. Until I can keep my demons in check,
I won't subject anyone I care about to them.

And I care about Lilah.

I don't know why or how it happened, but she means
something to me. I take a deep breath and yank my door
closed, then start the car.

When I walk into Sam Hill, Destiny's still on shift,
but Carol's already clocked in. I watch from the door as
Destiny passes the bar heading into the kitchen. She slips
behind the counter and clicks open the register.

I move along the wall to get a better look just as she
pockets what looks like two twenties from the register.

Her gaze flits guiltily around the bar as she slides the drawer closed…and connects squarely with mine.

I raise a brow at her and her eyes widen, realizing she's been caught.

Which explains why Ma's been riding my ass for my drawer coming up short most nights.

I shove my hands in my pockets and move toward her. "Money tight?"

She cringes and pulls the cash from her pocket. "We're short on rent."

"We?"

She nods. "Me and my sister just moved here and we haven't quite gotten our feet under us yet."

She tries to hand the money to me, but instead of taking it, I pull a pair of twenties from my wallet, replacing the ones she took. She just looks at me, trying to sort out what's happening.

"You need cash," I tell her, lifting the beer mug next to the register, "pull it from my tip jar."

She starts shaking her head, but I stop her by shoving a ten from the jar into her hand.

"This will keep Ma off my back. And anyway, since your sister's started playing here, my weekend tips are double, so really I owe you."

She looks at the cash, and I see the struggle in her eyes. Finally she pockets it. "Thanks. This will really help."

"Those cookies where really good, by the way. Were they from scratch?"

She nods and I sort of wish I didn't say anything when hope sparks in her eyes. "Glad you liked them."

But I brought it up for selfish reasons. "You should think about seeing if Molly needs some help over at Ambling Rose."

"The bakery?"

I nod. "She probably has more hours and the pay would be hella better than Ma pays her waitresses."

She tugs at the end of her ponytail and I'm all proud of myself for pulling that off with so much tact, until she says, "Ambling Rose is only open until four. Maybe when Carol goes on leave and I'm on nights here, I could do that in the mornings."

"Sounds like a plan," I say. It was an asshole move anyway. "I'll put in a word for you next time I'm there."

I'm a dick. It's the least I owe her.

She gives me a sparkling smile. "Thanks for the suggestion." She leans across the bar. "And whoever the lucky girl you're into is, I wish you the best of luck with that."

I nod, hoping she remembers she said that when she finds out it's her twin sister. "Thanks."

The two hours between when Destiny leaves and when Lilah shows feel endless, and I keep rolling how to approach this over in my mind. I *am* going to tell Lilah I'm into her tonight. I'm just not sure exactly how far I should take it. My stiff cock every time I think of her is all the indication I need of where I *want* to take it, but my better judgment tells me bedding her right off the bat is likely not the best strategy.

Because in my mind, this isn't a one-time thing. For the first time I can remember, I'm thinking beyond the first fuck.

But when she finally comes in and I see her crossing the bar toward me, I'm not sure I'm going to be able to keep my libido in check for another night. Because the fantasy of throwing her onto the bar right this second and sinking my cock into her consumes my every thought.

I slide a tip jar across the bar as she sets her guitar on her regular stool and unpacks it.

"I don't need a bodyguard," she says without looking at me.

"Good, because I don't know any."

Her eyes lift to mine, cold as a steel blade. "I can take care of myself. I've been doing it for years."

I nod. "I'm sure you can. That's not the point."

"Then what *is* the point?" she snarls.

I lean across the bar. "The point is, I want to walk you home."

She throws her hands up, exasperated. "I told you, I don't need you to!"

I lower my voice and let every ounce of desire I feel for her flow through my next words. "But the question is, do you *want* me to?"

I know she gets my message when her eyes flare and her face flushes. My eyes skim down her tight shirt and, as if on demand, her nipples harden for me. Her mouth opens to answer, but closes again as she climbs onto the stool. She pulls her guitar into her lap and starts playing.

A small group seats themselves at the booth nearest the door and Carol brings their drink orders to the bar. I'm mixing when Lilah's voice filters into my head, a song I've heard before but can't place. But the lyrics grab my attention and when I glance up at her, her eyes are burning through me.

It's a song about wanting something you can't have. When she hits her stride in the chorus—a verse about how fighting base instinct is futile—I feel my groin tighten in anticipation. If I'm reading this right, she's answering my question. And it's exactly the answer I was hoping for. She's feeling it too.

I mix her rum and Coke and slide it across to her. When she finishes her first song, she downs most of it before launching into the second.

Carol comes for her tray. "She's in rare form tonight," she says with a tip of her head at Lilah.

"Meaning?"

She turns her back to Lilah and mutters, "Meaning you two should just jump each other in Vicky's office and get it over with."

I scratch my head. "That obvious?"

A devious smile kicks up one corner of her mouth. "I could be blind and still see it."

In between orders, I try to stay busy with cleaning and inventory so I don't burn a hole through Lilah's skin before she even finishes the first set. I keep her glass full of Coke, but otherwise leave her be.

When Marcus, my ex-roommate, shuffles through the door with his girlfriend, I breathe a sigh of relief for the distraction. They arrange themselves around the table nearest the door and just as I round the end of the bar the door opens and his sister Blaire and her husband come through.

I knuckle bump Marcus. "Thought I was rid of you."

He shoots me a grin. "Caiden defended his dissertation today up at the Sierra State. I used the excuse to tag along for a Sam Hill burger."

I look at Blaire's husband as he settles into his seat. "How'd it go?"

He leans back, loops his arm around Blaire's shoulders. "They didn't ream me right on the spot, so that's something. I've got some clean up but nothing major."

"I don't really get all that academic shit," I say, lifting my hand for a knuckle bump, "but congrats, I guess."

He bumps me. "Thanks."

I turn my attention to Marcus's girlfriend, Addie. She worked here for a week a few months back, but I knew her before that because she had to retrieve her drunk dad off my barstool more than once. "How's Bruce?"

I'm glad when a small smile quirks her mouth. She wouldn't have smiled at that question even a few months ago. "Good. He's got a job and he's dating my aunt."

I feel my eyes widen. "Becky?"

Her smile grows into a grin. "That's the one."

"Wow, that's…great…?" My eyes tighten in a question. "Right?"

She nods. "I think so."

I take their drink order and head back to the bar just as Lilah finishes her set and lays her guitar aside.

"How long have you been playing?" I ask, as I pour Marcus a Bud.

"Since I was five." She runs a finger lovingly along the neck of the guitar. "This was my grandma's. She taught me to play and gave it to me when she got sick."

"Sick?" I ask, working on the rest of Marcus's order.

She nods. "Cancer. She died five years ago."

It makes me think of Grandpa and my 1970 Ford Torino—my most cherished possession. It's the only thing other than my family I truly care about, and that's because it's basically a member of my family too. That's how Lilah treats her guitar.

I get the tray for Marcus's table ready. When Carol comes by I give it to her and turn to Lilah. "Your grandmother would be happy you've taken good care of it."

She barks out a sardonic laugh. "The only reason it's not a pile of ashes right now is because I abused it."

I look a question at her.

She takes a deep breath and holds it before blowing it out. "My parents were tweakers. They blew up our house in San Francisco cooking meth. It burned to the ground along with the neighbors' houses on either side. We lost everything—" She lifts her guitar. "—but this. The day before the fire, I was trying to write something that wasn't coming out. I yanked on a string and it broke. A friend of mine was restringing it when our house burnt."

"You write your own music?"

She nods. "Don't play it much, though. It's not what people want to hear, so doesn't work out great for tips."

"Play me one of yours."

She gives me a sultry half smile. "I'm on break."

God, that smile, that voice. She's all sex. To take my mind off how much I want to fuck her, I turn the subject back to something less sensual. "Everyone got out of the house before it burned?"

She nods. "I guess the cops had been watching our house for a while. They hauled my parents off to jail as soon as they arrived."

I feel my eyes widen. "How old were you?"

"Fourteen," she says, then looks at me like she's expecting a reaction.

"That must have been rough."

Her gaze sharpens to a point as she scowls at me. "Like I said, I've been taking care of myself for years."

I suppose that explains some of the strength I sense in her. When she came back into the bar last night because of Poser, she wasn't particularly frightened. She just figured she's wait the asshole out, like it was a matter of better safe than sorry. She's sharp and smart with an edge of toughness about her that makes her fucking irresistible.

When I realize how hard I'm getting, I ask, "Are your parents still in jail?"

It's a little scary that talking about her parents blowing up the family home and going to prison barely helps to curb my raging boner.

She nods, her expression stone cold. "Three more years."

"Sorry."

Her laugh is bitter. "Why? I'm not. They got what they deserved."

There's obviously no love lost between she and her parents. I'm not gonna lie and say I'm not curious, but I want her to want to tell me. When she's ready.

"Were you close with your grandmother?" I ask instead, with a nod toward her guitar.

Her face softens and right there I have my answer. "When Destiny and I were little, Grandma would come pick us up in the city when school got out and we'd spend the summers at her place. It was on the ocean near Mendocino and there were these amazing tide pools we'd hike down the cliff to. My best friend Lo came with us most summers because she doesn't have any family. I wanted Grandma to come live with us when she got too sick to stay at home. I wanted to take care of her." Her face hardens and becomes sad. "But my mom said she was too much to handle and they put her in a nursing home."

"That's when she taught you to play?" I ask, hoping to lighten the suddenly dark mood hanging over her. "When you were at her house for the summer?"

"Me and Lo both. She tried to teach Destiny, but all she cared about was the boy next door. Pretty sure she lost her virginity to him the last summer we spent at grandma's." Her eyes snap to me and she cringes when she realizes what she said. "That was probably too much information. Destiny really doesn't sleep around."

I lean on my elbows and reach into her eyes with mine. "Destiny can fuck anyone she wants. That's her business, not mine."

She swallows and pulls her guitar into her lap, but her gaze burns back into mine as she plays. That voice reaches into me and grabs right onto my cock. Strokes. Makes me hard for her.

Carol comes by with Marcus's burgers. I give the bar a quick once over to be sure everyone's set, then grab my beer and follow her to their table. I pull an empty chair around from the next table and drop into it.

"So, how's Blaire's couch working out for you?" I ask Marcus.

"It folds out into an actual bed, dude," he answers through a mouthful of burger, and I see there are two on his plate. No surprise there.

"You've always been a overachiever," I say to Blaire. Both she and Marcus were class valedictorians, he two years after I graduated and she the year after that.

She lifts her hand to high five her husband. "Yep, really shot for the stars, didn't we babe? Living large in a one bedroom dump in the worst section of Oakland with a foldout couch in our rat infested living room. Doesn't get any better."

Caiden chuckles as his palm meets hers. If there's ever been a couple who have had a tough row to hoe, it's those two. He went to jail for fucking her when she was seventeen, and it was a year before he could come within fifty yards of her without getting his ass hauled back to prison. I was overseas during all that, but Marcus filled me in on all the gory details when I got back. He felt like Caiden had taken advantage of Blaire and wasn't happy they were together. But he had to eat his words when he met Addie. She was a member of his Oak Crest High water polo team and he basically lost his coaching gig because he couldn't stay away from her.

Moral of the story, don't fuck underage girls.

No worries there. I toss a glance over my shoulder at Lilah and find her watching me as she plays. Destiny has to be at least twenty-one or Mom couldn't have hired her to waitress. Good thing about twins is, that means I know how old Lilah is too. Not that I was worried. No question in my mind that Lilah is all woman.

I listen to the song she's singing and let her voice works its magic on me. And as the words sink in, I realize it's the first time I haven't at least recognized the song. I look more closely at her face and her eyes spark, and that's when I realize.

She's doing what I asked. She's singing something for me that she wrote.

I turn and listen to her sing about breaking rules and taking what you want. That voice combined with those words makes me want to climb right out of my skin and into hers. Before I realize she's done it, like some fucking snake charmer, she's pulled me right out of my chair with nothing but that voice.

CHAPTER 8

Lilah

Every time Bran's eyes rake over me, I catch fire and have to remind myself of all the reasons this can't happen. But I'm sure there has to be a wet spot on the back of the little black skirt I stole out of Destiny's closet when I was getting ready tonight.

Which proves I'm the worst person who's ever lived.

In my mind, I keep telling myself "hands off" when it comes to Bran. I've set my resolve that nothing can happen, despite the way I ache for him. When I changed out of my warm-ups and baggy T-shirt into some of Destiny's most revealing clothes before I came here, I justified it by telling myself it ups my tips. That's not a lie. But the second I saw Bran standing behind the bar, his black Sam Hill T-shirt clinging to his cut torso, I knew in my heart who I'd dressed for. At the wolfish spark in his eye when he saw me, the image of him taking these clothes off with his teeth flashed through my mind and I've been wet ever since.

My heart pounds every time I look at him—every time I catch him staring back. And I can't keep my eyes off him.

He's at the table near the door with two couples when I clear my throat and start on a song that I just wrote this week. It's still a little rough around the edges, but he asked to hear one of my original songs, and if there's a song I'm going to sing for Bran, it's going to the one he was the inspiration for.

He turns and looks at me, and at first it's the same predatory gaze he seems to reserve just for me. But as I start on the chorus of his song, and he hears what I'm singing, his eyes widen.

"There's nothing left to lose. There's nothing else to find.

Take my invitation, leave none of me behind.

Rules restrain the meek, and chains are meant to bind.

Inhibition broken, I'm crossing every line."

He stands and moves toward me, his eyes asking the question. I nod as I start into the next verse. His smile is so fucking sexy, it's everything I can do to remember to move my fingers on the strings. And the second I hit the last chord, he's got my arm and is dragging me off the stool. My guitar is still in my hand as he pulls me through the swinging door to the kitchen and halfway down a short hallway in back. He yanks me into a dark office and before I can process what's happening, my guitar is banging off something hard and Bran's strong arms are lifting me off the ground by the waist. As my eyes adjust to the dim light, I see he's set me on a desk. I lean my guitar against it as Bran wedges himself between my knees.

"I want to fuck you worse than I've ever wanted to fuck any woman, but right now, I'll settle for the taste of your mouth."

His lips crash into mine and the rush is intense. Every hair on my body stands on end at the feel of his hot mouth doing everything it can to devour me. He forces my mouth open with his and his tongue invades my deepest recesses. And it's like somewhere deep in my mouth, he's found my sex autopilot button. Without my permission, my hands fist into the hair on top of his head, and my knees spread and lift over his hips, causing my skirt to ride up my thighs. The moan that escapes my throat is low and feral, and I know he hears it when he grabs my ass and pulls me against the bulge in his jeans. There's only the thin cotton of my panties and the denim of his jeans between us as I grind the sweet spot between my legs against his hard length. He groans into my mouth as his fingers dig into my skin, and he grinds harder against me. His hand slips under my shirt and cups the swell of my breast, teasing the tight nub of my nipple with his thumb. The action sends shockwaves directly to my groin.

I've never felt this desperate. This willing. His hand glides down my stomach and I open my legs as he tugs my skirt out of the way. I reach for the button of his jeans and just get it undone with shaking hands when there's a loud bang from behind me.

"Oh, shit!" Carol gasps. "Sorry."

I cringe but don't turn around.

I expect Bran to let me go, but he keeps his grip on me. "Quiet out there?" he asks over my shoulder.

"Yeah. Only one table left and I just topped off their beers. I was going to clock out if you've got the bar."

He peels one hand off my ass and grabs the card out of the rack on the wall that says Carol on the top. "Got it," he says, swiping it through a machine next to the rack.

"Thanks." I hear the door hinges creak as it starts to close. "Night, Lilah."

"Night," I say, still too mortified to turn and look at her.

The second the door clicks shut, Bran kisses me again, slow and deep. "I've got to get back out there. Stay till closing."

"I can't." This is bad enough without Destiny asking me why I'm late. I have to be home by curfew.

His eyes burn into mine. "You can, because I'm taking you home tonight and I'm going to fuck you until you're screaming my name and can't remember yours. And then I'm going to fuck you again and again until the sun comes up."

He lets me push him back and I slide off the desk and straighten my skirt. "I can't."

His eyes soften and trace the lines of my face. "That song. What was that?"

I shrug and wipe the remnants of our kiss off my mouth with the back of my hand. "Just something I wrote."

"Sounded like you were fucking me with your voice," he says, his own rough with desire. "That's the part I heard loud and clear."

Then he heard what I wanted him to. I was brave enough to do that to him with my song, but I'm not brave enough to follow through with my body.

The pad of his thumb glides over my lips and his eyes flare heat into mine. "That voice of yours is pure sex. You've got to know that every time you open your fucking mouth, I get hard for you."

Damn. He knows just what to say to make me gush into my panties.

"I have to go," I say, grabbing my guitar by the neck and moving to the door.

He follows and slams a palm against the door when I reach for the knob. As he leans across me for the doorknob, his voice rumbles low in my ear. "You've already given me blue balls for a week. Don't make me wait until Friday to fuck you, Lilah."

This is spot in the script where anyone who truly loved her sister would tell the twenty-something man her sister wants that she's only sixteen. He should know the truth. It would solve the entire problem. As soon as he knows, he'll quit wanting me.

But God, I love the way he looks at me. The heat that radiates out of his gaze every time it finds me melts me from the inside out. In his eyes, I'm sexy and strong. I'm a woman. *His* woman. He wants *me*. The intensity of his kiss…the desperation in the way he ravaged me on that desk, as if I were his last breath. In all my life, nothing has ever been as empowering as the pull I have over him. Nothing has made me feel so plugged in and alive. One sentence out of my mouth would douse the inferno and bring whatever's happening between us to a screeching halt.

But I'm not ready to give up that feeling just yet.

So, because I'm such a selfish bitch, I instead of telling him the part of the truth that would turn him off, I give him the part I know will only turn him back. "I can't be with you, Bran. You slept with my sister and she's still into you. She's all I have." I glance over my shoulder at the desk, my stomach suddenly sour at what we just did there. "This was a mistake." I push past him and he lets me.

"This is going to happen, Lilah," he says to my back, "because you want it to."

I throw my guitar in the case and swipe the entire tip jar off the bar and shove it in my bag. I bolt for the front door and when I look back, Bran is just coming from the kitchen. He sends me a salute, as if he's anything but totally in charge.

Sergeant Seduction.

And I am the pathetic plebe who's in way over her head.

This is going to happen...because you want it to.

He's wrong. I don't want him. I *need* him. Like oxygen.

How the fuck am I supposed to resist oxygen? Even for the sister who's given up everything for me.

CHAPTER 9

Bran

I watch her go, but then remember the pervert poser. With Carol gone, I can't leave the bar, so I pull out my phone and dial.

"What?" Lilah snaps when she connects.

"Where are you?" I ask.

"Why?"

I blow out a frustrated laugh. This woman yanks me around like no other. "Just humor me."

"At the end of the block."

"People on the sidewalk?"

There's a pause. "Not really."

"Is that a yes or no?"

"No."

"Keep your eyes open and keep walking," I tell her.

"What's going on?" she asks, her irritation with me usurped by a thread of worry.

"I'm walking you home."

A sigh blusters through the connection and I can almost hear her eye roll. "I told you I can take care of myself."

"Then think of it as a favor to me."

"You worry too much."

I smile when her voice is softer, like a caress through the airwaves. "How far from your apartment are you?"

"Another block."

"Can you see your door?"

"Not really. The streetlight at that end of the block is out."

"Since when?" I ask, my skin prickling as my natural alarm system kicks in.

"I don't know. A few days ago, I guess."

"Do you have your key out?" I ask.

"Not yet."

"Get it out and have it ready when you get there. I don't want you fumbling for it at the door."

"Wow, you're really paranoid, aren't you? Is that a skill they teach you in the Marines, or does it just come naturally?"

I'm an inch from bolting out of this bar and tracking her down. "Just do as I say."

"Chill, Captain Caution. I've got my key in my hand."

"Eyes on the sidewalk, and especially the storefronts and doorways," I tell her. "And also, enlisted guys don't get to be Captains in the Marine Corp."

"Major Mayday?"

"Pay attention to your surroundings."

"Sergeant Suspicion?"

"How far are you?"

"Almost there," she says, the tease leaving her voice.

"Your key is ready?"

There's a pause and the sound of scuffling. My heart skids to a stop in my chest. "Lilah!"

"Inside," she says. "Locking the door behind me."

I release the breath I was holding and will my heart rate out of the stratosphere. "Don't be a stranger."

"Good night, Bran," she says, and then she's gone.

It's another hour before the last group leaves and I lock up. I cash out my drawer and bring it back to Mom's office. Everything's shoved aside from the spot where Lilah's ass was an hour ago and I run my hand over the smooth steel. She was everything I knew she'd be, honey and fire on my tongue and a volcano under my hands. I harden at just the memory of her.

But my first instinct was right. I shouldn't have pushed her. Problem is, my second instinct, my libido, is definitely in charge when it comes to anything to do with Lilah. My balls ache just thinking about that tight body pressed all up the front of mine, clawing at me and grinding that hot wet pussy hard against my rock solid cock. What I told her is true. She wants this, and if she can get past the shit with her sister, it's going to happen.

But I need to be more patient.

I take my last sweep of the place, shutting off lights as I go, then set the alarm and pull the front door closed behind me as I step onto the sidewalk. But before I turn, something hard comes down on my skull. I stagger and bright stars flash in the dark. I spin and the sidewalk tilts. In the second I fight for balance, a fist cracks off my jaw, knocking me back half a step.

"Not so fucking tough without your tanks and RPGs, are you baby killer?"

Blood trickles into my eye from my scalp and I wipe it away. But I don't need to see to recognize Poser's voice.

"Is he crying?" another voice says just as a baseball bat swings through the dark toward my face.

I duck and grab the arm holding it, flinging whoever it's attached to hard against the side of the building with a heavy thud. Someone grabs my arm and yanks. I lift my elbow sharply at the blurry face and hear a satisfying crunch as bone connects with bone.

"Fuck!" the second voice screams, and the form in front of me collapses in a heap.

I blink to clear my eye and see Poser pull himself up from the sidewalk. His partner in crime is hunched on the sidewalk holding his face. Blood gushes between his fingers from the vicinity of his nose.

"I suggest you take off," I say, getting my bearings and standing straighter.

Poser's fists tighten at his sides and he holds his ground, but his buddy's not so sure. He gains his feet and blinks at Poser, blood running down his face and dripping from his chin. I take the opportunity to elbow him again.

He screams as he turns and runs for a red sedan parked just down the street.

"Don't you fucking think about it!" Poser shouts at his retreating form, but the coward doesn't even slow down. He flings himself into the car and the tires squeal as he peals out.

Poser gives me one last glare, then leaps into the road. His buddy slows, but doesn't stop, and Poser rips open the back door and scrambles in.

Only after they're gone do I rub my head. The goose egg is already enormous. "Fuckers," I mutter as I head up the block toward the Torino. I give her a quick once over and she looks unscathed, so I guess they didn't know which car was mine. I tug my T-shirt over my head and wipe my bloody hands with it before pressing it to my head. Sweat and tears, absolutely, but no way I'm bleeding on my car.

When I get home, I pull into the carport and just sit here with my shirt pressed against my head, waiting for the bleeding to stop. When it does, I duck under the hood of the Torino, deciding she needs new plugs.

I contemplate calling the cops, but it's not like they're going to post anyone on the bar. In the end, I decide

Poser's not enough of a man to finish what he started. I doubt he'll be back.

But there's no fucking way that Lilah is ever walking home alone again.

At the thought, my mind goes to Ma's office and all that sweet, wet heat in her mouth and between her legs. And when the sun comes up, I'm covered in grease and no closer to understanding how Lilah Morgan has me so twisted around her finger. All I know for sure is, I hope she never figures out how to untwist me.

CHAPTER 10

Lilah

Bran's texted me twice since Saturday. I ignored him. But I can't stop thinking about that kiss. It's been four days and I'm still on fire.

I feel like I should be grossed out, kissing someone my sister has slept with, but the sick knot in my stomach has nothing to do with being grossed out and everything to do with knowing my willpower won't last forever. The high I got from letting myself go with Bran was more intense than any drug I've ever tried. I feel the draw of addiction pulling at the root of me, demanding that I feed it. Now I know firsthand why Destiny's holding out for Bran. He's a drug that, once you've had a taste, is impossible to quit.

But I have to. Even if Bran never wants Destiny the way she wants him, I can't do that to her.

Luckily, for the last two nights I've had a distraction. Lo made it through the Knockout Round last week. Monday and yesterday were live performances. She sang P!nk's "U + Ur Hand" and kicked ass on the performance show last night, but now that it's down to the final twenty, it's live shows and audience voting, so it gets a little dicey.

Tonight is the Wednesday results show, and I settle into the corner of the couch and say a prayer to the music gods that she makes it through before clicking the remote. But the second I do, there's a bright flash, then the screen goes dark.

"No!" I cry, bolting to my feet. I jab the remote at the TV and punch the power button at least a dozen more times to no avail.

Destiny skids to a stop in her bedroom door, panic in her eyes. "What's wrong?"

I move to the TV and bang my fist against the side a few times, because that's what Dad used to do when his shit didn't work. "*The Voice* starts in two minutes and the stupid TV won't turn on!"

Destiny blows out a relieved sigh. "You scared the living shit out of me. I thought someone broke in or something."

I throw a hand at the TV in exasperation. "It's *The Voice*."

She comes over and takes the remote from my hand. She clicks the power button then slaps the side of the TV. Apparently, we both learned electronics repair at our father's knee. "Tiffany said it was on its last legs when she gave it to me."

It, along with the double bed mattress and box spring in Destiny's room and the kitchen table, were cast-offs from her friend, Tiffany, who had extra stuff to get rid of when she moved in with her boyfriend.

I glance at the clock and fresh jolt of panic catapults me toward the door. "I need to find a TV. Right now."

"Where are you going?" Destiny calls as I yank the door open.

"Sam Hill!"

I fly down the stairs and nearly face plant into the door at the bottom when I lose my footing on the second to last stair. I catch myself and on the frame before I hit it because Bran is right. The rickety thing would blow right off the hinges without much provocation. I close it behind me and make sure it latches, then sprint toward the center of town.

Bran is leaning on the bar talking to Carol when I slam through the door. Both their heads pivot around when the door bangs off the wall. I instantly understand why he suggested I only come in on weekend nights when my wild glance flicks toward the TV and finds the tables between me and it totally empty. There is a guy on a barstool and a couple in the corner booth and that's it. I blink at the episode of *Ink Masters* that's playing and rush up to the bar.

"You okay?" Bran's eyes flick past me to the door, looking for the stalker, no doubt.

"No!" I pant. But that's when I see the shiner under his right eye and the purple bruise that the thick scruff on his jaw can't fully hide. "What happened?"

He looks at Carol.

"She needs to know the truth," she coaxes.

He takes a deep breath and his eyes find mine again, boring through me with their intensity. "Poser and his buddy ambushed me at closing Saturday. I need you to take me seriously when I tell you to be vigilant."

My eyes nearly pop out of my head and before I can think better of it, I'm touching his face. For the briefest second, his eyes flutter shut as my fingertips trail along his bruised jaw line. "Oh my god. Are you okay?"

"I'm fine, but those guys are fucked in the head, Lilah. I wouldn't put it past them to try something. Promise me you'll let me walk you home."

"So they can do that to you again?" I say, my heart lodging in my throat. "No. I won't."

"They blindsided me," he says with a solemn shake of his head. "My mistake. One I won't be making again."

"Listen to him, Lilah. He can handle those guys," Carol says with a jerk of her thumb at the door. "But what he couldn't handle is if something happened to you."

Bran cuts her a sharp look.

She shrugs and turns for the couple in the booth. "Just calling it how I see it."

"What are you doing here?" Bran asks me, irritation bleeding into his words. I'm not sure if he's irritated at Carol or me, but either way, I feel a jolt of panic when I remember why I came.

"Turn it to *The Voice*!" I realize I'm yelling when Carol and the couple she's talking to turn and looks at me. I feel my face scrunch in embarrassment. "Please," I beg, lowering my voice several decibels. "My TV broke, and it's the results show. I can't miss it."

"*The Voice*," Bran says, one thick, dark brow arching skeptically.

"Please," I implore.

He looks the question at me a moment longer before reaching under the bar for the remote. He flips channels until he finds it, then clicks off the stereo and un-mutes the TV.

I hike myself onto a barstool and breathe a sigh of relief when the warm up band is still playing.

"Why all the urgency?" Bran says from behind me.

When I turn to look at him, he's sliding a glass across the bar toward me. I take a sip and find it's my standard rum and Coke. "My best friend is competing."

His eyes widen. "On the show?"

I nod. "She's kickass."

He glances up at the TV and smirks as the intro band wraps up. "On *The Voice*."

He doesn't believe me. "Google her. Her name is Shiloh Luck. She's from San Francisco and she's the only contestant to turn all four coaches' chairs in her blind audition. She's going to win."

"That's what it would say if I Googled her?" he says, his voice full of amusement. "That's she's going to win?"

"If it doesn't, they don't know what the hell they're talking about."

A smug smile lifts one corner of his mouth as he leans onto his palms. "Then why are you so worried about missing the results show? You already know what's going to happen."

"Shh!" I say as Carson Daly's voice pulls me back to the TV.

I hear Bran chuckle behind me, but my eyes are glued to the screen as the remaining contestants are called up to the stage. My heart stalls in my chest when I see Lo lead the rest of the group into the spotlights. She's dressed just as kickass as she sounds when she sings, in a strappy top, short ruffled skirt with sequins, and high boots. Her copper afro is tamed into tight corkscrews and her coffee-with-too-much-cream skin glows in the stage lights. She's the smallest one out there, petite and at least three inches shorter than anyone else, but there's no way anyone notices that. All she's doing is standing there, and she's got the biggest stage presence of the group. Even Carson Daly fades in her presence.

They mess with the stage lighting and cue the dramatic music. The atmosphere goes all suspenseful as we wait for him to name the first artist through to the finals.

When he says Lo's name, my heart skips and I drop my head back in relief. She hugs the girl next to her and I wonder when she turned into a hugger. That's new.

They cut to commercial and I sag in my seat, totally relieved.

CHAPTER 11

Bran

"Congrats," I say, then take a swallow off the beer I just poured myself.

She turns slowly and looks at me. "Thanks."

My eyes flick toward the TV. "Is that the friend that went to your grandma's with you…the one you played the subway stations with?"

She nods. "All she had to do was open her mouth and people would stop and listen. My guitar case was always full of bills after just a few songs."

"Well, the producers must have thought there wasn't much suspense in keeping the audience hanging, or they wouldn't have pulled her first."

"I'm telling you, she's going to win. Everyone knows it."

I look at her a long second, her silver eyes stirring up my insides and turning them electric. Finally, I lean across the bar. "I want to kiss you again."

She draws a shaky breath then swallows half her drink. "I told you, I can't."

She turns her attention back to the TV when the intro music for the show starts. The host announces the next act, Shiloh and two other contestants singing "Renegade."

I watch Lilah, rapt with attention, a smile twitching her full pink lips as her friend sings. But I don't hear anything up there that can touch what Lilah does with her voice. When Shiloh's group finishes, Lilah drops against the back of the barstool and grabs fistfuls of her platinum hair. "Oh my god!"

"You're better," I tell her.

She straightens up and whips around, glaring me down as if I've slapped her. "You don't know what the hell you're talking about."

I shrug. "I may not know a whole lot about music, but I know what I like."

She throws a hand at the TV screen in frustration. "She opens her mouth and anyone who hears her shivers. She hits a note and it sinks right through you and lodges in your soul. Her voice imprints on your DNA so you can never forget it. *No one* can do what she does."

"I disagree." I lean on my hands, pressing closer and lowering my voice. "Because none of those things happened to me when I heard her sing, but they *all* happen every time I listen to you."

Her lips part as her face flushes, and for several beats of my heart we just stare at each other. Finally, she shakes her gaze loose from mine. "I should go home."

"Not without me."

Her gaze sharpens to a point and snaps back to my face. "I'm *not* taking you home, Bran."

I haul a deep breath and blow it out. "I meant, I'm walking with you. You know, safety in numbers and all that."

Her eyes soften as they trail over the damage to my face. "I can't believe he..." She lifts her hand and I want so badly for her to touch my face again, but she lowers it and grabs her drink instead. She polishes it off in one long swallow.

I lift the rum bottle. "Another?"

She shakes her head, but she's not looking at the bottle. Her eyes are fixed on my mouth. As they trace the lines of my lips, I feel that shiver she was talking about. I feel her gaze wrap itself around the deepest part of my soul and lodge there. I feel her presence weave into my DNA and know I'm never going to forget her.

No one's ever done anything like this to me.

Every cell in my body is rioting against my head. My every instinct is to throw her on the bar and sink my cock balls deep inside her.

But I have to slow this train down. When I fuck her, it's going to be because she begged me to.

"Carol!" I call across the bar, where she's now sitting in the booth with the couple.

She looks up.

"You got the bar for a few?" I ask with a nod at Lilah.

She waves a hand at the door and a smile ticks one corner of her mouth. "Take your time."

"C'mon," I say to Lilah, coming around the bar. "Let me walk with you." When her look grows wary, I hold up my hands. "The next time these are on you, it will be because you put them there."

She nods and starts toward the door.

When I determine the sidewalk is empty, I scan for the red sedan. "I don't care if it's day or night, I don't want you walking around out here alone."

She starts toward her apartment. "He was pissed at you for making him look like the fool he is." Her gaze finds my face as I keep step next to her. "He made his point, so I doubt he'll be back."

"Maybe you're right, but I'm not going to chance it," I say, casing the block ahead as we cross the street. "Call me if you have somewhere to go and you're alone. I'll come for you."

"For how long?"

I stop and pin her in my gaze. "Until I know he's gone."

We walk, and my eyes are everywhere: in every alcove and recess of the storefronts we pass, behind us, ahead of us. Everywhere but on her.

But I feel her.

Every time her gaze flicks over me, it sends pins and needles over my skin and causes my breath to catch. When we reach her door, she's already got her key out. She twists it in the lock and the door whines as she pushes it open. She steps up onto the landing at the bottom of the narrow stairs and turns back to me. We're eye to eye and I feel hers draw me to her, like magnets for my soul.

But I need more than that if I'm going to touch her again. I need her to reach for me first.

After a long, electric moment, she backs a step deeper into the gloom of the stairwell. "Good night, Bran."

"'Night."

I wait for her to close the door, then test the knob. I still don't like how flimsy the door is and I make a note to order her a steel security door at the hardware store tomorrow morning. I cross over to the other side of the street and head back to the bar. And when I glance back, Lilah is standing in the second story window, watching after me.

CHAPTER 12

Lilah

I fall asleep in eighth period algebra. Of course, I only know I'm sleeping when the bell rings and I wake with a start. The pencil in my hand goes flying and hits the football jock who sits in front of me in the back of the neck.

He rubs the spot and turns to smirk at me. "If you wanted my attention, you didn't need to stab me in the neck. A tap on the shoulder would have worked."

He's reasonably hot, longish blond waves and blue eyes a few shades darker than Destiny's. But he knows it, which makes him exponentially less attractive in my eyes.

I gather my things and shove them into my bag, and find he's still watching me when I'm done.

"I'm Jon," he says, handing me back my pencil.

"Lilah." I shove the pencil into my messenger bag, then hike it onto my shoulder and start for the door.

He bounds up next to me before I reach it. "You coming to the Homecoming game tonight?"

"Wasn't planning on it."

I keep moving toward the front doors and my escape. I haven't seen Bran since he walked me home Wednesday, and I was hoping that two days would get me past whatever this infatuation I have with him is. But every night as I lay in bed, instead of the memory of his kiss fading, it's set down roots and blossomed into much more. In my dream last night it progressed to its logical end, and as he sunk his thick length inside me, I came hard. It woke me out of a sound sleep and I lay quiet for a long moment, afraid I'd woken Destiny with my cry of pleasure. If he can do that to me in my sleep, I don't even want to know what would happen if I let him touch me again in real life.

So I can't.

I skip down the three marble stairs to the sidewalk and find Football Jon still on my heels. "You should go to the game. There's a dance after."

"Don't do dances."

He shrugs as he lopes along beside me like a big, gangly puppy dog. "No one really dances. We just hang out…hook up or whatever."

I look at him again, closer this time. "Are you asking me to the dance so we can 'hook up or whatever'?"

A lopsided smile pulls at his inordinately large mouth. "What would you say if I was?"

It's Friday. I still haven't found an after-school job, so I need to play tonight.

"Busy, sorry."

His eyes light up. "But if you weren't...you would have said yes?"

I think about that. Hooking up with a guy my own age might get my mind off the ex-Marine with the soul as dark as his eyes. A soul that speaks to mine in a way no one else's ever has.

I stop and fix Jon in my gaze. This puppy dog is clueless. He hasn't lived through anything that's shaken his sense of safety and challenged him to define his place in this world. He's like a whim...a child with the emotional depth of a mud puddle.

The polar opposite of Bran.

"Yes," I say, telling him the truth. If I didn't have to play, I'd go to the dance, see where it led. If it led to me forgetting about Bran for a few hours, then all the better.

A grin pulls his mouth wider than should be humanly possible. "So, change your plans. Come to the dance with me."

I start up the sidewalk again. "I can't. I've got a sort of job I need to be at."

His brow creases in confusion. "A sort of job?"

"I'm looking for a real job, but this one's temporary until I find something else."

"What sort of hours you looking for?" he asks.

I shrug. "My sister's making me go to school, so it would have to be weekends or afternoons."

He looks at me, those puppy dog eyes full of curiosity. "You wouldn't be in school if your sister didn't make you come?"

"No. It's pointless."

"Huh," he muses, scratching his head. "Never really thought school was a choice."

"That's the problem. It's not. I looked into getting my GED, but you have to be eighteen and within six months of when you'd have graduated if you stayed in school, so…" I flick my wrist up the hill toward school. "Here I am."

He's still scratching his head, as if his motor program got stuck. "What about your parents? They don't care if you're in school?"

I huff out a derisive laugh. "They're in jail because the only thing they cared about was getting stoned."

His eyes widen and his hand drops. "Oh."

When I realize we're nearly to the bottom of the hill I glance at Jon. "I haven't seen you walk home this way before."

He gives his head an exuberant shake. "I have football practice after school. My car's in the lot."

"Then what are you doing here?" I say with a wave toward town.

He grins. "Getting a date to the Homecoming dance."

I stop and heave a sigh. "What time is the dance?"

His hand goes back to his head and scratches, and I realize he really is part puppy. "After the game, so around nine thirty."

"Can you pick me up?" I ask, knowing if I don't have a ride, Bran will insist on bringing me.

He gives me that same manic nod. "Where?"

"Downtown, at Sam Hill Saloon. You know where it is?"

His nod gets more exuberant and his grin pulls wider. "I'll jump in the shower right after the game and come for you around ten?"

I lift my brows at him. "Should I feel special that you're showering for me?"

His expression tugs into a comic grimace. "You don't want to smell me after I come out of that uniform."

We reach the fringe of town and I can see the end of the block where our apartment is. I guess Bran would be happy I didn't walk home alone.

Jon's feet slow. "I gotta get back. We've got a team meeting and Coach will have my ass in a sling if I'm late."

"Ten," I say.

He grins and nods again, and I wonder that his head doesn't fly from his neck.

"I need you to wait for me in your car." I want Bran to know I'm going out with someone else—maybe cool his jets a little—but I'm not quite ready for him to know it's a high school guy. "I'll find you when I'm done. What do you drive?"

"White mustang. I'll be out front."

"Good luck at the game." I turn and head home without looking back.

I'm at the bar by seven and spend the next three hours trying to ignore that Bran's gaze is burning me alive.

When he lifts the rum bottle on my second and third refills, I nod. I've never done a high school dance and I'm really dreading it. But I need this…a distraction. A little before ten, I go to the bathroom to straighten myself up, then head back and start packing.

Bran comes around the bar. "It's early. Where are you going?"

"I've got a date," I answer without looking at him.

"A date." It rolls out of his mouth and thuds heavily onto the bar between us.

I tip my head at him. "Is that a problem?"

He takes a deep breath and holds it, as if to steady his temper, before blowing it out. "You can date whoever you goddamn please." He leans closer and his voice purrs in my ear. "But when you're done with your playthings, you *will* come looking for me."

I laugh and try to keep the shake out of it. "The size of your ego is staggering."

I down the last of my rum and Coke, grab my tips from the jar, and head to the door. Parked at the curb is a shiny new white Mustang with the headlights on. I duck down as the window rolls down.

"Hey, beautiful," Jon says, pushing my door open.

I slide my guitar into his backseat and climb in, and as we pull away from the curb, I look back and find Bran watching from the door.

"How was the game?" I ask, hoping he didn't see my shudder.

"Won easy."

I roll up my window. "Great."

He smells good, like soap and some decent cologne. He's in a hoodie and jeans, and he really is pretty good-looking. The rum has loosened me up some and I decide this is going to be okay. Maybe even fun.

When we unload in the parking lot, he ushers me toward the gym. "You okay hanging with my friends?" He gives an exaggerated eyebrow wiggle. "Or were you wanting me to yourself this evening?"

Oh, god. I hadn't thought about friends, but if the alternative is leaving him with the impression I want to be alone with him, they're the lesser of two evils. "We can hang out with your friends."

We slip through the door into the gloom of the gym and he pulls me over to the corner near the locker rooms.

"Tyler and Cameron," he says, pointing to a pair of guys hovering there in the shadows. "They're on the team too."

I follow half a step behind as he heads their direction. "Guys, this is Lilah. Lilah, the guys."

The larger of the two, with deep set eyes and what appears to be a perpetual frown, nudges his chin at me. I look from him to Puppy Dog Jon and wonder how they're even friends. The other one, a wiry guy with a bad haircut, reaches into his sock and pulls out a flask, offering it to me. "Tyler."

Jon takes my hand and pulls me behind them to the corner. I take the flask and smell. Whatever it is smells nasty. I take a quick sip and hand it back, trying not to make a face. Each of the guys take a long swig.

"Here you guys are!" a girl's voice squeals over the music. I turn and find two girls coming toward us from the dance floor, sweaty, out of breath, and holding hands.

The rounder of the two, with short dark hair and huge boobs, takes the flask from Jon's hand and chugs, then hands it to the pretty Asian girl she's with. She's a little shyer about it, only taking a small sip.

Tyler grabs her long black hair and tips the end of the flask higher. "C'mon, Amy. Live a little."

A dribble spills down her chin and Tyler licks it off then kisses her. He backs her into the shadows at the side of the bleachers and pins her against the wall. Her fingers weave into his hair and they don't look like they're planning to come up for air for a while.

Jon's arm slips around my waist. "So, that's Amy, Tyler's girlfriend, and this is Melissa. She's with Cameron."

Cameron already has his hand possessively on her ass. "Hey," she says with a wave.

"This is Lilah. She's new." He tugs me closer and shoves Cameron's shoulder. "I scooped her up before any you assholes could fuck with her."

"A regular fucking Clark Kent," Cameron mutters. He goes over and grabs the flask from Tyler's hand. Once his hand is free, Tyler instantly starts groping the front of Amy's shirt. Cameron hands the flask to Melissa. "Wanna get out of here?"

She takes another drink and nods.

"What about you guys?" he asks Jon.

Jon looks at me. "Want to go party?"

I shrug. "Sure."

Cameron shoves Tyler. "Come on, asshole. We're heading up to Lover's Leap."

We all file out of the gym and are warned by the Leadership kids manning the door that there's no re-entry.

Jon knuckle bumps one of them, a cute blond girl. "See you at home, sis."

I glance over my shoulder at her as we pass and see the family resemblance. "What year is she?"

"Senior," he answers with a squeeze of my waist.

"What about you?"

He looks at me. "Sophomore, same as you...right?"

I shake my head. "Junior."

His eyes widen. "Thought everyone in algebra two was a sophomore."

"I missed some school, so I'm a little behind on math."

His mouth pulls into that exaggerated grin. "You just got so much hotter."

I roll my eyes and let him load me back in his car. We follow two other cars up a long winding road into the mountains. There's barely a moon tonight, so it's pitch black when we get to a clearing and everyone cuts their lights. We pile out of our cars and Jon leads me to a path that winds out to a rocky outcropping. Everyone finds a seat and Jon settles against my side.

Tyler's flask has been replaced by a full bottle of Johnnie Walker, and everyone takes their turn. When it comes to me, I take a swallow and it burns all the way down.

The guys shoot the shit about the game and their girls talk about some other girls that I don't know. I tip my head back and stare up at the ocean of stars overhead. I'm just getting dizzy when I feel warm wet lips on my neck. I lift my head and realize the chatter has stopped. Tyler and Amy aren't anywhere to be seen, but Cameron has Melissa flat on her back with his hand down the front of her shorts.

I look at Jon and he raises his eyebrows at me. "If you want to."

I shrug. "Sure, why not."

He closes the few inches between us and his mouth finds mine. His kiss is wet and sloppy, his tongue lapping at mine like a Labrador Retriever. So, now at least I know what breed he is.

We kiss for a while, and his hands never leave my waist. I close my eyes and wait for something to happen—a buzz in my chest or an ache or tingle or *anything*. All I feel is a wet tongue in my mouth that's not mine.

When Cameron and Melissa start getting loud, Jon stands and pulls me up by the hand. "Let's take a walk."

I brush my ass off. "I should probably head home. I've got a midnight curfew."

He holds my hand and we move slowly back down the path toward where we parked, but when we get there, Tyler's doing Amy on the hood of his car.

Jon takes a deep breath and opens his car door for me. "Sorry about them."

"It's cool," I say, dropping into his passenger seat.

He climbs in the driver's side and looks at me, a spark in his eye.

"For them," I qualify. "Don't get any ideas or I'll have to bust out the Kung Fu."

"You know Kung Fu?" he says, his eyes going even wider.

I shake my head at him. "You don't want to find out."

He starts the car and we wind back down the mountain, past the high school toward town.

"So, where did you come from?" he asks.

"San Francisco."

He glances sideways at me. "Sort of a big change, huh?"

"Yeah. My sister thought this would be better for us. It's cheaper to live here and all."

He slows where he turned back to the high school this afternoon. "You'll need to navigate me from here."

I point straight ahead. "I'm in the first block, on top of the gun shop."

He coasts down the hill and rolls to a stop in front of the gun shop. "Look, Lilah, I know this was kind of lame, but maybe we can see a movie or something sometime."

I step out of the car and close the door, then rest my arms on the door when he rolls down the window. "Maybe."

He unbuckles and leans across, waiting for a good night kiss. I lean in and press one to his lips. He grins like the fool he is as I draw away.

"You need to learn the finer points of kissing," I say. "You're really bad at it."

"You're going to teach me?" he asks eagerly.

"Good night, Jon," I say, but he just keeps grinning.

I stand and cross the sidewalk to the apartment door. Once I have it open, I give Jon a wave. As he pulls away, he passes an old black car that shines under the streetlight just up the block. There's a man leaning against the fender, his arms crossed tightly over his chest.

A jolt of adrenaline sends me backpedaling through the doorway…until I realize who it is.

Bran.

A shiver runs up my spine and my nipples harden. I tell myself it's the late-night November chill, but I know that's a lie.

I drop my guitar and storm out my door and across the street. He doesn't move until I'm right on top of him, and then it's only to push off the car and stand in front of me.

"What the hell are you doing here?" I demand.

His eyes scan me head to toe. "I wanted to know you were safe."

I shove him back against his car. "So you're *stalking* me? That doesn't make me feel safe. It makes me feel like worms are crawling under my skin. It's fucking creepy."

He nods slowly. "You're probably right."

I sigh deeply. "You're going to have to trust that I can take care of myself, Bran."

He glances up the street in both directions. "I care about you, and that pervert is out here somewhere."

I ignore the dizzying rush in my chest from his declaration and fist my hands on my hips. "So this has nothing to do with my date?"

His jaw grinds tight, and that's all the answer I get.

I lift my hand slowly, cup his cheek and run the pad of my thumb under his black eye. "Thank you for caring, Bran. I appreciate your concern. But this can't happen. You know that."

You know that.

I say it, but I know he doesn't "know that." And the reason he doesn't is because a huge part of me doesn't either. I don't mean it and he can sense that.

He lays his hand over mine, holding my palm against his warm skin.

I lift my other hand and hold his face in my hands. He watches me, letting me decide what happens next. I feel like my heart's being pulled up my throat. It's beating so hard for him.

I lean in, needing to feel what I felt when he kissed me. Needing to feel that spark lighting my dark soul. But just before our lips touch, I lower my gaze.

He rests his chin on the crown of my head and sighs deeply into my hair. "You smell like whiskey."

I let his face go and back away. "I'll see you tomorrow, Bran."

He nods and watches me cross the abandoned street.

When I walk through the door and the lights are on, I have a moment of panic that Destiny was watching for me to get home from my date and maybe she saw me with Bran just now. But she's nowhere near the windows. Instead, she's hunched on the couch, her face in her hand, talking on the phone.

"I don't know, it just got all jerky and then the engine died and it wouldn't start again," she says to whoever's on the other end. There's a pause while they reply, then she says, "That sounds bad. How much do you think it will cost to fix?" Another pause, then a dejected, "Shit" at whatever the answer is.

She cringes up at me as I lower myself onto the couch next to her. I wait through the rest of the conversation and surmise that she was talking to Tiffany's boyfriend when she asks him to put Tiffany back on. She swears a few more times, then says her goodbyes.

"The car?" I ask when she disconnects.

She sets the phone down. "He thinks it could cost up to a thousand to fix. We're barely scraping the rent together as it is."

"I'll find a job after school. There has to be something." I give her shoulder a mock punch. "I bet no one's got the corner on underground gambling at the high school yet."

Her head snaps up and panic skates over her features.

"Joking." I twist the ends of my hair around my finger. "Mostly."

"You are *totally* joking. No gambling here, Li."

"It was good money," I mutter.

She rolls her eyes. "You're impossible."

"Thank you."

She gets up and pours herself a glass of water. "How was your date?"

I decide to skip the part about his friends being oversexed drunks, because it doesn't really seem to apply to Jon. "It was nice."

"Define nice," she says warily.

"We just went to the dance and hung out with some of his friends. Sort of boring, but okay."

She moves through the living room to the hallway. "I'm wiped out. See you in the morning."

I follow her up the hall when she's done in the bathroom, then crawl into bed. And the kiss I replay in my dreams, the one that has my breathing ragged and my heart erratic, isn't Jon's.

It's Bran's.

CHAPTER 13

Bran

I thought I was fine with Lilah fucking anyone she wanted...until I saw her leave with that asshole. I've never held a woman to any standard. No such thing as sluts or whores in my book. A woman likes to have a good time, more power to her. If she wants to have a good time with me, even better.

But watching Lilah drive off with that guy tore something inside me loose. I felt the hole, just like when I lost brothers overseas. It was that same deep ache that won't go away. But I can't even begin to explain why I'm feeling it for a girl I've only known for a few weeks.

All I know is, every time she walks through the door, it takes me a sec to get my bearings. Her own private gravitational field yanks at my compass and fucks me all to hell. And when she opens that pristine mouth and fucks me with her voice, there's nothing I can do to stop my body from reacting.

But the next few weeks pass and I keep my hands off. It helps that it's the brink of December and the weather's getting cooler, so she's starting to wear more clothes. It also helps that I've discovered three feet is my breaking point. If I keep her at arm's length, I can't smell her. Because just as much as she sounds like sex, her warm vanilla scent smells like it too. I don't text or call. There's been no sign of Poser and the dick in the white Mustang has been picking her up after work. I haven't gotten a look at him, but he seems to treat her okay, so I haven't needed to stalk her or walk her home.

In her eyes I'm probably as pathetic as Destiny is in mine. I told Destiny this wasn't happening and I couldn't understand why she didn't believe me...until I realized I was doing exactly the same thing to Lilah. She told me no, but I haven't let up believing it would happen.

It's finally sunk through my thick head, though. It's not like Lilah and I had a thing. It was a kiss. As mind-blowing as it might have been, it wasn't like I thought it was heading for anything serious.

So it's time to saddle up and move on.

When Lilah comes in tonight, it's the same as every other Friday and Saturday night since our kiss three weeks ago. I mix her drink, set out her tip jar, and leave her alone. She sings and makes me hard for her, just like every night, but unlike all the others, tonight I decide to do something with all that wood.

In the corner is a table of five college girls out trolling on a Saturday night. Two of them have been checking me out since they walked in. I make sure they see me checking them out in return, and when they're due for a second round, I mosey over. I lay my hand on the blonde's bare back and squeeze the brunette's shoulder. "Anything I can get you girls?"

The brunette licks her shiny lips and looks at her friends. "Are we staying for another round?"

They all nod and she lays her hand over mine and looks up at me. "I'm not driving tonight. Switch me to a Long Island Iced Tea?"

"Sure thing, doll," I say, giving her shoulder another squeeze.

"It's my twenty first," the blonde says, batting her long black lashes up at me. "I want something that tastes good with lots of liquor."

Her friends giggle and start throwing out suggestions like Sex on the Beach and Fuzzy Navel.

"I've got just the thing," I tell her with my cockiest smile.

She smiles back. "I trust you implicitly."

I arch an eyebrow at her. "You might want to reconsider that, doll. Trusting me could lead you down a very questionable path."

Her lips part and she just stares at me for a long second before saying, "I'll totally follow."

And just like that, I know who I'm taking home tonight.

I go back to the bar and mix their drinks, and when I let Lilah's voice filter into my consciousness, she's nearly ripping the strings off her grandmother's guitar. I take a second to settle the adrenaline she always stirs in me before looking up at her. She's watching me with narrow eyes and a glare as hard as the steel of her eyes.

I pull my gaze away, unwilling to let her derail my plan. She's out fucking White Mustang, so I'm not going to let her make me feel guilty about taking what I need too.

Instead of leaving the tray for Carol, I bring the drinks to the girls' table. I dole them out and hand the blonde hers. "Let me know what you think."

"What is it?" she asks, taking a cautious sip.

"Just something I came up with."

"So we should just call it Hot Bartender?" the brunette says, brushing her fingertip over my arm.

The girls all laugh and the brunette winks at me.

So, now I'm thinking threesome, and I'm also thinking this might not be able to wait until I can get them home.

"This is really good," the blonde says, and everyone decides they need to have one too.

I go back to the bar and start mixing. Lilah finishes her set and lays her guitar aside. When my eyes find hers, there's anger and frustration, and something else I can't read.

"You may as well just fuck them right on their table," she spits.

I pour gin into the shaker and start shaking. "I'm thinking about it."

"And what about Destiny?"

I slam the shaker on the counter and pierce her with my gaze. "What about her?"

When she glances around the bar, I realize several people are watching us, including the college girls. She comes around to my side of the bar, grabs my elbow, and tows me through the swinging doors into the kitchen.

"She's in love with you," she says, throwing a hand at me. "How can you do this to her?"

Jeff's giving me a shit-eating grin from the grill and I roll my eyes. I turn for Mom's office and Lilah follows me.

"She's not that stupid, Lilah. I don't know what's going on inside her head, but love isn't anywhere in the equation. Just like you told me this wasn't happening," I say, waving a hand between us, "I told her. It just took us both a while to get it."

The muscles in her jaw flex. "You're a total shit, you know that?"

I press my lips together and nod. "Yep."

She hangs her head. "Why do I even care?"

I sit on the desk. "That's what I'm trying to figure out. You're off fucking White Mustang, so why does it make any difference who I fuck. And don't give me some bullshit about Destiny."

She lifts her head and looks at me, and her expression is totally indecipherable. There's a storm in those darkening eyes that makes me think she's on the edge of blowing her top, but her face is pale and her lips are parted as though anticipating something.

She slams into me before I even know she's coming, and she starts clawing at my neck and back, as if trying to climb right into me. It takes a second for her mouth to find mine, but when it does, her kiss sucks every ounce of air from my lungs and leaves me desperate for my next breath.

Which is her.

My next *everything* is her.

We devour each other, hands, mouths, bodies clashing together in a hurricane of desire and need, devastating everything in its path.

In some back recess of my brain, I'm vaguely aware that someone is saying my name, but it's lost in the cyclone of the feel and taste and smell of Lilah. The sound of her moans.

A steel hand grabs my arm and yanks. "Bran!"

Lilah gasps and pulls away, and my vision focuses on Carol's red face.

"What?"

"My water broke. I need a ride to the hospital."

I look down and her leggings are dripping onto the floor. "Jesus!"

"Vicky said she's getting dressed and she'll be here in fifteen to cover the bar. We need to go."

"What about Wyatt?" I ask, finally gaining my wits.

"He took Isaac up to his parents' for the weekend to give me a break. It'll take him over an hour to get back."

I turn to Lilah, who's still staring at me, stunned speechless. "Can you keep an eye on the bar until Mom gets here?"

She nods.

I push through the office door and Jeff's prepping a tray of nachos. "Lilah's watching the front," I say, whisking Carol through. "Mom will be here in a sec."

"We got it covered," Jeff says with a nod at Lilah. He's fifty and married, but I feel a stab of jealousy at his gesture and realize just how screwed I am.

But thankfully, I've got a crisis to keep me from delving too deeply into exactly what Lilah means to me. I'm trying not to hyperventilate at the image of having to deliver this baby in the backseat of the Torino.

When Carol and I reach the sidewalk, Mom is just climbing out of her car. She's in her PJs with her hair up in rollers.

"Let me take her," she says, opening the passenger door for Carol. "It makes more sense for you to stay here."

"You don't have to ask me twice." I guide Carol to her passenger door.

"I thought you were changing," Carol says as I lower her into Mom's car.

Mom pokes at her curlers. "Decided my grandniece was more important than my image." She waves before she drops into the driver's seat. "I'll keep you posted."

I watch them roll away from the curb. One bullet dodged.

But there's another waiting at the bar to take me down.

I take a deep breath. The night air is cold and helps ground me. Because, despite everything that just happened with Carol, it's that kiss that's left me spinning.

Inside, Lilah is standing at the end of the bar, looking every inch as stunned as I feel. She just stares at me a long second before climbing onto her stool. "You didn't make her drive herself, did you?"

I smile. "Mom just got here and took her."

I pick up the drink shaker with the girls' concoction and pour it into glasses, then bring them to the table. They all thank me and the blonde slips a napkin into my hand. When I look, I see it's got her number scrawled on it. But I can't find it in me to follow through with what I started.

Lilah's playing when I get back to the bar. She doesn't look at me and I'm not sure what that means. And at eleven thirty, same as every other night, she packs up.

"'Night, Bran. Hope everything's okay with Carol."

I nod and she leaves. And out the window, a white Mustang passes by.

CHAPTER 14

Lilah

Jon's family is scarily well adjusted. He's got an older sister, Jennifer, who's the cheerleader I saw at the dance, and a younger brother, Jeff, who's in junior high. His parents are both home from work by six every night and they eat dinner together as a family, late on practice days and early on game nights. I've never seen anything like it, even on TV.

We've spent a lot of time together in the three weeks since the Homecoming dance. He drives me to school, and picks me up on his way home from practice every Tuesday and Wednesday so we can watch *The Voice* together, because our TV still isn't fixed. On Fridays, he picks me up at the bar at eleven thirty, and on Saturdays, he drives me both ways.

But we've only kissed three times, and they've all been at school, when his friends were watching. And that was all the week after the dance. Over the weeks between, things have evolved into something very un-romantic. We sit and bitch about teachers, and his friends, and he talks about his love of all things Marvel, which makes sense since he's a little comic himself. He's turned out to be not so horrible to hang out with.

We're sitting at the dinner table and everyone's taking turns talking about their day. The only one who seems to escape show-and-tell is Jon's dad, who just sits at his end of the table chewing and nodding at what everyone else has to say.

When they all look at me I feel myself tense a little. I can sing to a crowded room, but there's nothing I hate more than talking about myself. "Nothing really happened at school except the algebra test Jon mentioned."

"How do you think you did?" Bethany, Jon's mother asks, all bright eyes and smiles.

I shrug. "Pretty sure I bombed it."

Her face goes all mock disappointment. "Maybe Jonathan can help you study for the next one. He's a math whiz."

I don't tell her he helped me study for *this* one. Don't want to tarnish his "math whiz" status.

She pats my hand. "I was talking to one of my dearest friends today, and her brother's family runs Mimi's, the market on the corner of Main and Sierra. She said he might be looking for stock clerk if you haven't found anything yet.

"That would be great. Thanks!" I wonder to myself if there's an employee discount. Destiny and I are barely scraping by and something for dinner other than ramen would be nice every once in a while.

She tells me who to ask for when I stop by and we move on to Jeff.

He talks about his soccer team as we all finish eating and clear the table. When the kitchen is clean—another family activity—Jon and I head to the loft where the kids' TV is. It's Wednesday night. The semifinals results show. *The Voice* is down to its final six and Lo is one of them.

I'm totally wired as we settle into the couch, and Jon loops his arm over my shoulders to keep me from bouncing off the walls. I'm used to it by now. He's a touchy feely guy and we spend a lot of time like this.

The show starts and my eyes are glued to the screen as the remaining contestants perform in groups. In between, Carson Daly announces who's safe and who's not. They're down to the last two and they still haven't put Lo through, and when they finally call her name, they bring her up with the other contestant and tell us one is safe and the other will have to sing for her survival.

And then they cut to a fucking commercial.

I scream right out loud and Jon throws his hand over my mouth, laughing. When he stops laughing and his rubber lips pucker up, I realize just in time where this is going.

"Whoa, there, cowboy," I say, lifting my hand and pressing it against his face. "You'd take advantage of a girl in a compromised mental state?"

He shrugs. "It's been a while. Wanted to try it again."

I roll my eyes. "That's so romantic."

He looks at me for a long moment. "You don't put a whole lot of stock in the reputation thing, do you?"

I'm not sure if that's an insult or a compliment. "Meaning?"

He shrugs and watches the talking lizard on TV try to sell us insurance. "You don't seem to care much about what other people think of you. That's really brave."

"If you say so."

"How do you do that? Not care?"

I look at him again, just now picking up on the fact that he *does* care, and maybe wishes he didn't. "What's going on?"

He takes a deep breath and unhooks his arm from my shoulders. He watches his hands fidget with the remote as he lowers his voice and says, "I'm not sure I like girls."

I take a second to process that before I slip the remote out of his hands and pause the TiVo. "You mean you don't *like* them? Like…you like boys better?"

He shrugs. "It's just something I've been thinking about."

"Have you ever tested your theory out?"

He cracks that goofy smile. "I was just trying to, but my test subject rejected me."

I kiss him, no tongue, but long and slow. "Anything?"

He shrugs. "It's nice."

"But no…zing." I wave at his privates.

He makes a face. "Not really."

"What about the guys you know? Have you...I don't know, tried doing anything to see how you feel?"

"I haven't kissed a guy or anything, but I'm pretty sure I want to."

"Have you talked to anyone about this...a counselor or whatever?"

He shakes his head.

"Why are you telling *me* this?"

He presses his shoulder into mine. "So, this is where it gets a little weird. I've only known you a few weeks, but I feel like I've known you forever. But I don't think the guys I really *have* known forever would take this very well, so...you're the safest." He tips his head and looks me in the eye. "Plus, you don't really know anyone here, so it's not like you're going to blab it around, right?"

"Right." I slouch into my seat and flick a wrist between us. "This all kind of makes sense now."

He takes my hand and squeezes. "I meant what I said about you being hot. I figured if there was any girl who'd do it for me, it would be you."

I press my forehead to his. "Thanks. I think."

He takes the remote back and starts the program, fast forwarding to the part where Lo and the other girl are standing holding hands, shoulder to shoulder, waiting for their fate.

And again, I wonder when Lo got so touchy.

They've already dug every ratings point out of the human interest angle of Lo being a foster kid and never knowing any of her blood relatives. All the stupid jokes have been made about long lost relatives coming out of the woodwork after her notoriety on the show. So instead of beating that dead horse, Carson Daly asks them both a lame question about their inspiration.

When it's Lo's turn to answer, she says. "My best friend Lilah has been through hell. She's incredibly talented and she should really be here instead of me. Every night when I get up on stage and sing, I'm channeling her. I'm doing this for her."

"Holy shit!" Jon says from beside me. "That's you, isn't it?"

All I can do is nod.

And a second later when Carson says, "Congratulations, Shiloh! You and your friend Lilah are through to the final," I scream again.

My phone buzzes in my pocket just before Jon and I reach the doorway of our last period algebra class. I fish it out of my pocket and my feet stall when I see it's Lo. She's been so crazy busy I only hear from her every few weeks. She called the week before last to ask me if I'd written anything fresh. Said some of the contestants had written their own music for the original song performance and she hoped they'd let her use one of mine. I sent her my newest—the one I wrote for Bran—but never really thought it would fly with the producers.

"It's happening, Li!" she shrieks in my ear when I connect. "They loved your song!"

My heart skids to a stop and I can't answer.

"Li?" she says, her voice cautiously irritated. "This isn't your fucking voicemail, is it?"

"No," I finally manage. "I'm here."

"I can't do this without you. I got you and Destiny tickets for the final. They're in the family section, right up front."

My heart skips. "Oh my God, Lo! Are you serious?"

"You have to get your asses to L.A. by Tuesday afternoon. Please! I can't sing your song without you here."

"I'll be there." I change direction and head for the front doors, my heart pounding.

"Gotta go, Li," she says, "but this is going to be so fucking epic!"

She disconnects, but I realize I'm jogging down the hall with my phone still pressed to my ear when Jon calls after me. "Where you going? Algebra is this way!"

"I'm going to L.A.," I squeal, waving my phone in the air.

As I cross the parking lot and start jogging down the hill toward town, I remember that the damn car is broken. I slow and Google bus fares from Oak Crest to L.A. My heart sinks when the numbers pop up. One twenty round trip. Times two, and that will take everything I make this weekend. Maybe more. Destiny will never go for it.

Destiny's on shift at Sam Hill, so I head straight there. When I stumble inside, there's an older woman behind the bar. She's graying, a swirl of white through her long, dark waves, but her dark eyes are Bran's. I glance around and find Destiny standing at the end of the corner booth, taking orders. I move toward the bar and slide onto my regular stool to wait for her.

"Let me guess. Lilah?"

I look at the woman behind the bar. "Hi."

She smiles. "You will never be able to deny your sister. You two are nearly identical."

I shrug. "Mom has strong genes."

"I'm Vicky," she says, extending an arm across the bar. "I've heard all about you."

"Don't believe anything Destiny says," I say, smiling and shaking her hand.

Her eyes flash mischief. "It's my son Bran who can't stop talking about you."

The smile falls off my face and my heart holds its breath. "What does he say?"

"Nothing specific, except that I should hear you sing. But the fact that he talks about you at all is impressive. Bran's not a talker."

"Hey!" Destiny says from behind me. "What are you doing here? School's not out yet."

I turn as she hands her order across to Vicky. "Lo got us tickets to the finals. We have to go to L.A. on Tuesday."

Her face falls. "Lilah, we have no car."

"I checked on the way over. We can take the bus."

The faintest hope lights her eyes. "How much?"

I try not to cringe. "One twenty each. I'll make that this weekend."

She cringes for me. "Li…we need that money for the car."

Panic seizes my heart at the realization that this might not happen. "This is once in a lifetime, Destiny! My best friend is about to win *The Voice*. I have to be there for her!"

"Who's doing your car repairs?" Vicky asks.

I turn and find her pushing Destiny's full drink tray across the bar.

"It's over at D'Amico Brothers," Destiny answers.

"What's he quoting you?"

"Six fifty," Destiny says. "It needs a timing chain."

Vicky scratches her head. "I dated Wayne for a while. Let me talk to him and see if that's the best he can do. If you can come up with the cash for the parts, he might let you make payments on the rest."

"God, that would be amazing. I'm totally good for it." Destiny looks at me. "We could probably come up with a hundred a month if we're careful."

"Would we have the car by Tuesday?" I ask hopefully.

Destiny's face crumbles. "They haven't even ordered the parts yet because I wasn't sure if we could afford to pay for the work."

So nothing about Vicky's solution gets me to L.A. I drop my forehead onto my folded forearms.

"I'll try to think of something, Lilah," Destiny says, rubbing my back.

I lift my head. "I'll give up my phone."

She shakes her head. "I need mine, Li, and yours is only an additional twenty bucks a month. Giving it up won't save us much."

This can't be happening. "I'll hitchhike."

"Oh, hell no," Vicky says, and when I look up, she's at the tap, pouring a beer. "Way too many rednecks and methheads out here."

Destiny and I look at each other with the word methhead. There are plenty of those where we came from too. Our parents being two of them.

Vicky moves down the bar toward her customer and I bolt off the stool, panic fueling my need to move. "There has to be a way! I have to go!"

"I'm sorry, Li," Destiny says with a cringe. "The timing's just really bad."

It's Thursday. I've got five days to figure out how to get to L.A. Jon has a car. But I deflate at the certainty his parents would never let him skip school to take me. I could seriously get the gambling going at school like we did at Wells High, but that was really Lo's thing, and five days isn't enough time to make any serious bank anyway.

The press of hot tears tightens my throat, but I swallow them back. Crying is useless and stupid and only serves to make sure everyone knows exactly how weak you are. I don't cry. Ever.

But, despite my resolve, I feel my eyes dampen. I turn and shove through the door before anyone notices. When I run smack into a solid wall of cement on the other side,

I look up through blurry eyes at six foot plus of dark-haired brood.

Despite that I'm flailing for balance, I look away. Destiny seeing me cry would have been bad. Bran seeing it is worse.

He grabs my arms to steady me. When he lifts my chin, I close my eyes. The action forces a tear pooling in the corner over my lashes. He starts to thumb it away, but I yank out of his grasp and scrub it off myself.

His jaw grinds tight and those dark eyes glow death. "What happened, Lilah? Did someone hurt you?"

I shake my head. "No. Nothing like that. I'm fine."

His expression softens as his eyes scour my face for the truth. "I may not have women quite figured out, but I'm pretty sure when they leak it means there's a problem."

"I just had something in my eye," I say, pressing my knuckles into it.

He gives me a slow, skeptical nod. "Okay."

I'm usually a really good liar, but with Bran, all my wires get crossed and I forget myself. I blow out a defeated sigh. "Shiloh got Destiny and me tickets for *The Voice* final, but our car's in the shop and we're saving everything we can to get it fixed. We can't afford bus tickets."

"Where and when?" he asks.

I sniffle and wipe my arm under my nose. "Tuesday in L.A."

He glances at the battered wooden door to the bar. "Tuesday's are slow. Mom can cover the bar for me. I'll drive you down."

The flood of relief nearly drowns me. "Oh my god! Seriously?"

He smiles this heart-stopping smile. "Seriously."

Before common sense kicks back in, I spring into his arms. "Holy shit!" But then I realize where I am and draw back. "Sorry."

He lets me go, but his eyes burn into mine. "You've got nothing to be sorry for. I think I've made it pretty damn clear I'm good with you there."

I take a deep breath and chew my lip. "You should date Destiny."

He holds my gaze. "I've already told both of you that's not happening."

"Why?" I challenge, and I realize on the wave of frustration that word rides that I need to know if it's because of me.

"Either you're into someone or you're not. I'm not into Destiny. I shouldn't have slept with your sister. I knew that a minute after it happened. If I could undo it, I would. But if she's holding out some hope of a thing between us, it's because she didn't hear me when I told her it wasn't going to happen." He takes a deep breath and shakes his head. "The honest to fuck truth is, if I'd met you first, we wouldn't be having this conversation, because I would have taken you home that night, and the night after that, and every night since. I've never done a real relationship in my life, but you make me think it might be worth a shot."

It *is* because of me. I ruined this for my sister.

I shake my head and back away another step. "I'll check Amtrak."

His jaw tightens. "You're not taking the damn Amtrak, Lilah. Tell Destiny I'll bring you guys down and drop you at the studio. I've got a buddy from my unit down there. I can hang with him while you guys are at the show."

"Is this going to be weird? You, me, and Destiny?" I already know the answer before I ask. It's going to be excruciating.

He shrugs. "Not for me. I've got nothing to hide. I've been up front with both of you."

And I've lied to everyone. "Then you get the gold star."

He lifts my face with a finger under my chin and holds me in his intense gaze. "You tell me what you want me to do, Lilah. I'm not a great actor, but if you want me to pretend to Destiny that you don't light my fuse, I'll give it my best shot."

I shake my head out of his grasp, then keep shaking it, because lightning has struck me dead with the realization I'm totally falling for Bran. I know this because of the panic rising like a tsunami inside of me.

There's no way the three of us can spend hours trapped in a car without Bran finding out I'm sixteen. All

Destiny has to do is mention I'm missing school, or ask about making up my homework.

All along I've told myself I didn't care if he found out—that it was just a crush and when he ditched me, it wouldn't matter. But the way my intestines are tying themselves in a knot around my stomach is all the proof I need that I was lying to myself.

I'm falling in love with Branson Silo.

Shit on a stick.

I have to tell him the truth.

"She can't know I kissed you," slips out of my mouth on a wave of all-consuming panic. So much for the truth.

His eyes grow suspicious, and I realize it's because I'm coming totally unwound right here in front of him. "What's going on, Lilah?"

"Nothing." My head keeps shaking all on its own as I back away from him. "Nothing's going on. Just promise me you won't say anything to Destiny."

He holds up a hand. "I won't tell Destiny, but I think *you* should."

Oh, hell no. My head is still shaking. I can't stop it. "This is a bad idea." I turn and stagger toward home.

CHAPTER 15

Bran

With Carol out, Destiny's taken over nights this week. Last night she was lamenting that she needed to find a way to get her sister to L.A. for the show, so I know Lilah hasn't mentioned my offer.

I should leave it alone, but when Destiny clocks in for her Friday night shift, I pour her a Diet Coke. "Have you figured anything out for L.A.?" I ask as I push her glass across to her.

She shakes her head, all gloom and doom. "This is really important to her, but I just gave the guy at the auto shop all the money we had plus everything I stole from your tips jar to order the part for the car. We've got no spare cash."

I drum my fingernails on the bar and stop myself when I realize it's driven by nerves. "How would you feel about me taking you two down?"

She just blinks at me.

Lilah's going to hate me for this, but it's too late now. "Mom will cover for me here. It's really not a big deal."

Her eyes widen and her whole face lights. "It's a *huge* deal. Lilah's the only family Shiloh has."

"So…if we leave early Tuesday morning, that would get us to L.A. around one. Does that work?"

"I'll check with her, but I think so."

One of my regulars slides onto the barstool at the end and I start on his beer. "You should tell Mom you'll be off that day too. She can get my sister to cover the floor after she closes up the gym."

She shakes her head. "I can't afford the day off work, but you going with Lilah is perfect. Even if I could have come up with the money for a bus ticket, I was worried about sending her alone."

The comment strikes me as a little off until I remember what happened with their parents. I know Lilah worries about Destiny and that obviously goes both ways.

A shudder fingers down my spine and settles in my groin at the thought of an entire day with Lilah. "Sounds good."

I move down the bar and drop my customer's beer in front of him. He tells me about his gout and the twelve-year-old Indian doctor that his insurance has referred him to. I listen, but the whole time, in my mind, I'm alone in the Torino with Lilah.

And I'm watching the door.

Seven.

Eight.

Nine.

A knot forms in my chest.

The place is full and Destiny is tripping over herself trying to keep everyone happy. Carol always makes it look so easy. She comes up with an order and brushes a loose strand of hair back from her face. "Didn't realize how nuts it gets in here on weekend nights. No wonder Lilah does so well."

I grab at the opening like a drowning man at a buoy. "Speaking of, where is she?"

She pulls a face. "She got a job over at that corner market, but I think they close at eight."

I start on her order. "Didn't know she'd found something."

"Her boyfriend hooked her up."

Shrapnel cuts through my insides and my hands stop mid-pour before I force them moving again. I toss her what I hope passes for a casual glance. "They serious, you think?"

She shrugs. "They spend a lot of time together, so I guess."

I set up her tray and she heads back out to the floor. When Lilah's still not here at ten, I know she's not coming. Which makes me wonder again about her meltdown yesterday. I said something that spooked her. I've replayed the conversation over and over, and I'm still not sure what. Either way, I seem to have scared her off, which means she's not going to be happy I set Tuesday up behind her back.

CHAPTER 16

Lilah

Today was my first day at my new job. It doesn't pay enough that I can quit playing at the bar, but tonight was also the last home football game, so instead of Sam Hill, I went up to school after I got off at the market. I figured making half of one game was the least I could do for Jon, considering everything he's done for me.

There's a party in the park after the game that we stop by. He keeps his arm around me and I'm good with that. Drunken lust has set in and there are a few guys eyeing me. Jon on my shoulder is like full body armor, totally innocuous but enough to deflect an attack.

Finally, one of the guys comes over anyway, and that's when I realize it's not me he's checking out. It's Jon.

I'm surprised when Jon doesn't let me go to talk to him. If anything, he pulls me closer. They talk a little about the game and he tells Jon congrats on the win.

"The enemy," Jon says when he's gone. "Linebacker for the other team."

"He was cute."

Jon kisses my cheek. "Not my type."

My eyes widen. "Changing your mind?"

He shrugs. "Keeping it open."

My phone buzzes a little after eleven and I pull it from my pocket. Destiny.

"Thought you'd be at Sam Hill tonight. Where are you?"

"Decided to go to a party with Jon instead." Because there's no way I'm ready to deal with whatever my mutinous hormones have going on for Bran right now. Especially with Destiny for an audience.

"As long as everything's okay," she says. "Also, I have great news. I was going to tell you when you got here, but since you're not coming...Bran is going to drive you to L.A! How awesome is that?"

I feel that same electric jolt I felt when he suggested it. But I told him no. I think. The whole conversation yesterday kind of got swallowed by my panic attack and I don't really remember how it was left.

"Tell him thanks, but I'll figure something else out."

"Lilah," she says, exasperated, "it's four days away. I can't take the time off from work and I don't want you going alone. This is the perfect solution."

It is so far from perfect there's not even a word for how un-perfect it is. But then I really hear what she just said. "Wait...you're not going?"

"If we're going to be able to make those payments on the car, I can't skip a day."

I open my mouth to say I shouldn't go either, then, but I can't force the words from my mouth. This is the biggest thing to ever happen to me.

Well...the biggest thing that doesn't involve blaring sirens and the destruction of an entire city block, anyway.

I look pleadingly at Jon and he looks a question back. I've already asked him if he'd play hooky and he surprised me by saying he would...except they're in the middle of playoffs, and if he misses practice his coach would have his ass in a sling.

He says that a lot, which makes me curious about the boys' locker room. I picture slings hanging from the ceiling like something out of Christian Grey's red room of pain.

"Okay," I hear myself say.

"I'm so happy we found a solution, Lilah. I would have felt guilty for the rest of my life if we couldn't have gotten you there." There's a crash and the breaking of glass, then Destiny's "Shit!" through the line. "I've got to go," she says and the line goes dead.

Jon presses his forehead to my temple. "You look like you swallowed a porcupine."

"I got a ride to L.A. for Lo's final."

"AHH!" he wails banshee style in my ear, grabbing me with both hands and shaking.

"Yeah," I say, extricating myself from his grasp before he gives me whiplash.

"This calls for a celebration." He drags me to the keg and pumps the tap, then fills two cups. He hands one to me and holds his up ceremoniously. "To famous friends and their coattails."

I tap my cup against his. "So now *I'm* set. Who's coattails are *you* going to ride?"

That rubber grin stretches his mouth. "Yours."

When Jon drops me at the apartment, Destiny's still at work. I could probably stretch my curfew now that she's working nights, but I don't really feel the need.

But if Destiny's not even taking the day off to come to L.A., I can't justify quitting the bar. So, if she hasn't already spilled my secret, tomorrow I'm going to suck it up and tell Bran the truth: he's a chaperone, not a date.

CHAPTER 17

Bran

This is fucking torture. It's been two days since Lilah flipped her shit on the sidewalk and my mind has been blowing gaskets trying to figure out what made her come unglued like that. She's usually so composed. So confident. All kinds of scenarios are shuffling around in my head. Something with her boyfriend, maybe? Or maybe something from before, with the parents? But nothing really takes hold and forms into a solid possibility for her reaction.

All I know is she seemed suddenly younger and more vulnerable, the fear that Destiny would find out about us bringing out something childlike in her that I'd never seen there before.

And I know I didn't imagine it when she won't look at me when she comes in tonight.

Something's going on with her, and I'm not sure I'm going to like what it is.

Destiny's in the kitchen when Lilah slides onto her stool.

I mix her drink as she unpacks her guitar, then push it across to her and lean on my elbows. "So, you pumped for Tuesday?"

Her eyes flick to me then back. "I thought I told you I'd find another way."

I shrug. "Been looking for an excuse for a road trip. You're it."

She takes a breath so deep I'm surprised she doesn't burst a lung. "Look, Bran, there's something I need to tell—"

Destiny bursts through the kitchen door with a plate of chicken wings in her hand and cuts her sister off midsentence with a hug. "Hey! It's so awesome that we're here together!"

Lilah bumps her forehead against Destiny's and there's a warmth in her eyes I've never seen before. I've seen plenty of heat there—fire that made me hotter than the pits of hell—but this is different, and suddenly I get it. They're close.

Really close.

They're fucking twins, so I guess I should have known that, but it took seeing them together to drive it home.

All my insides cramp as the hard truth hits me. The second fucked her sister, any chance I had with Lilah was gone, even though I didn't know she existed yet.

And I've been a royal dick, pushing her to choose me over her fucking blood.

I brace my hands on the bar as Destiny flits across the room and drops the plate on the table under the window. As much as I'm not sure how, I know I've got to back the fuck off.

"So..." I say, pushing off the bar and drawing myself a beer. "I figure if we hit the road by seven, that will get us to L.A. in time to grab a bite and head to the studio."

Finally, Lilah really looks at me. "Seven. Got it."

"Unless you think you'll be able to hang out with your friend after the show, we should be able to be back on the road in time to get home by one or two."

She shakes her head. "She tried to get a minute, but she says she won't be able to hang out. They've got a car back to their hotel and then interviews and some taping for a commercial or something."

"Okay, then," I say with a nod. "Sounds like we have a plan."

She looks at me a long minute, like she has something else to say, but when Destiny comes back by, she gives her an unsure smile and strums the strings.

I try not to let her voice affect me. I've heard it enough now that I keep thinking I should be building up some kind of immunity, but I forget how that smoky timbre caresses me, and how the pitch vibrates every cell in my body and goes straight to my groin.

She so fucking owns me.

Destiny's busy enough that she doesn't spend much time just hanging out at the bar, and when eleven thirty rolls around, Lilah starts packing up.

"So, I'll come by your place Tuesday morning," I tell her as she latches her case.

She empties her tip jar into her bag. "Seven o'clock. I'll be ready."

And that's it. She finds Destiny for a hug on her way out, then she's gone.

CHAPTER 18

Lilah

The doorbell rings and I jump at the sound.

"That's him," Destiny says, setting down her coffee mug and coming around the counter. "Go. I'll call you in sick when school opens."

I hike my bag onto my shoulder and walk toward the door as if marching toward my execution.

She comes with me. "I'd come down with you, but I don't want Bran to see me with no makeup."

"It's fine," I say, pulling open the door. "He thinks we'll be back around one."

"Just shoot me a text when you leave L.A.," she says, pulling me into a hug. "You're in good hands, so I won't worry."

I nod and start down the stairs.

"And hey, Lilah?"

I turn and Destiny's sitting on the top step, her cheek in her hand. "It's a long ride, so if you get a chance to, I don't know, say something about how cool I am or whatever..." She trails off with a "you can't blame a girl for trying" shrug.

"Will do." I turn and head down the rest of the stairs so she can't see the guilt on my face.

"Take pictures!" Destiny calls after me.

At the bottom of the stairs, I stop and collect myself before opening the door to the street. When I do, Bran is standing there.

"Hey," he says. "You ready?"

I nod and he turns and leads me across the street to his car parked at the curb. I wait for him to click the locks, but instead he turns the key in the driver's door lock then slides in and reaches across to unlock the passenger door.

I lower myself into the car and look around. There are cracks in the black vinyl of the seats and there's a hole in my floor mat where it's worn through. But otherwise, it's spotless. No McDonald's wrappers or old Coke bottles rolling around on the floor like our Neon. "How old is this car?"

"It's a '70 Ford Torino. My grandpa bought it new back then, drag package and all." He gives the steering wheel a pat as he starts the car with the other hand. "She's a member of the family."

"Wow," I say, giving it a closer look. "And it still runs?"

He flicks on the headlights, hits the gas, and we rumble away from the curb. "It was our project the whole time I was growing up. Think I was five the first time he stood me on a stool at the side of the hood and told me if I learned to take care of it, it would be mine someday."

"He gave it to you?"

He watches the road ahead as he grips the top of the wheel tightly with one hand as shifts with the other, weaving us through the quiet of the early morning streets. "For my eighteenth birthday, a year before he died."

"I'm sorry."

He shrugs, his eyes still firmly on the road, but in the brightening light of the rising sun, his eyes glisten with a sheen of moisture. "Everyone dies."

There's an awkward silence and I look out the passenger window as we leave the fire station and the last of town behind. We wind down the hill, through a few towns that look just like Oak Crest, eventually finding the never-ending orchards of the valley.

"So...you're good with cars, then?" I finally ask as he negotiates us onto the southbound highway ramp.

"Learned a thing or two."

"Our car's in the shop. They're going to charge us six fifty for a timing chain. Does that sound right?"

He nods and flicks a glance at me. The first since we left home. "It's a big job. The parts are cheap, but you have to pull everything apart to get to it, so sounds like they're charging you for six hours labor."

"Yeah. That's what they said."

I only realize how dejected I sounded when he glances at me again. "You want me to take a look?"

I shake my head. "I just wanted to be sure they weren't ripping us off. We'll figure it out."

"Have you told Wayne to start the work yet?"

"I think he might have ordered the part."

"I'll have him tow it to my place."

My eyes widen and snap to him. "I didn't mean...I just wanted to make sure it we weren't getting ripped off."

"If you pay for the part, I'll take care of the rest."

The engine rumbles every time he presses the gas pedal, like some kind of wild thing, and it strikes me how perfect this car is for Bran. They both feel wild and a little dangerous.

He glances at me as he weaves through the loose Tuesday rush hour traffic and his grip on the steering wheel tightens. "How does your boyfriend feel about this trip?"

For a second, I'm totally lost.

He must see the bafflement on my face, because he clarifies. "White Mustang?"

I feel my eyes widen. "Jon."

"Jon." His lip curls in an acerbic smile as he repeats his name.

"He's not my boyfriend."

His eyes cut to me. "Does he know that?"

I nod. "Definitely."

"So, just a fuckbuddy?"

"Just a garden variety buddy. No fucking."

He shoots me a sideways look, then takes a deep breath and blows it out slowly. "Good."

"Why good?"

His lips press into a line and he shakes his head. I realize it's to reconsider the course of this convo when he changes the subject. "I think it's great that you and Destiny are so tight."

I scowl at him. "That was random."

He flashes me a glance. "Just an observation."

I settle deeper in the seat. "You have family other than Vicky?"

He nods. "My parents split when we were kids and Mom got the bar. Dad got the gym, which my sister Brenda runs. She and Ma live in town and Dad lives in Jonestown…so just far enough that he and Ma don't need to see each other all the time, but close enough they can get in each other's faces or beds—whichever mood strikes."

I can't stop my mouth falling open. "They sleep together?"

He shrugs. "Sometimes."

"You don't think they'll get back together?"

He blows out a laugh. "No. They hate each other."

"But they sleep together…?"

"It's complicated." He shoots me a glance, and in it, I see the fire he's trying so hard to contain.

I should tell him. I opened my mouth to say it at the bar on Saturday night, but then Destiny was there, and after she was gone, the moment had passed. I even typed it into a text last night, but then decided the fact he's been fondling a sixteen-year-old was something he deserved to hear from the horse's mouth.

I *will* tell him.

Right now.

"Mind if I play some of Lo's tracks?" I blurt, holding up my phone.

He opens the center console and pulls out a wire with a headphone jack. "It's the original stereo," he says with a nod at the dash, "but I rigged it."

I plug the jack into my phone and cue my Lo playlist. She's gotten the bonus bump on her score every week for hitting the top ten on iTunes.

I tip my head back and close my eyes as Lo's voice fills the car and transports me back to the subway. I can hear her pure tones echoing off the tile walls around us, drowning me in awesome.

When it gets to the end and starts to repeat, I click it off.

"Don't bite my head off, Lilah, but you're every bit as good as she is."

Bran's voice is low, and when I look at him, he's looking right back at me.

"Road," I say, pointing out the windshield.

He turns his eyes back to the highway that stretches straight and flat for as far as the eye can see. We're in the middle of nowhere, so there are very few cars, and none nearby.

"It could just as easily be you in the final tonight."

I huff a frustrated laugh through my nose. "You don't get it. Shiloh is special."

His arm straightens, pushing his shoulders deeper into the seat. "So are you."

CHAPTER 19

Bran

With just that one sentence, she totally closes off. Her arms fold hard across her chest and she turns to look out the passenger window. She's so angry that I suggested she might be better than her friend.

"Why are you afraid of that?"

She turns back to me. "I'm not *afraid* of anything. It's just not true."

I've seen the look on her face a thousand times in Afghanistan—sometimes when I looked in the mirror. It's the expression we all wear when we're desperately trying to convince ourselves we're not afraid. But our eyes always betray us, and I see her fear shining there.

I shake my head. "*Everyone*'s afraid of something."

"What are you afraid of?" she shoots back.

"Wow," I say, gripping the steering wheel a little tighter. "Where should I start?"

She just looks at me, waiting.

"I'm afraid of dying before I've ever lived. I'm afraid the best is behind me and this is all there is. I'm afraid of missing out on something great because I didn't recognize it in time to grab hold. I'm afraid of admitting that I want more, because what if there isn't more?" I grip the wheel and look at her. "I'm afraid of falling asleep."

"Nightmares?" she asks.

I look out over the endless road. "Not if I don't sleep."

"Tell me about them."

Cold sweat breaks across the back of my neck and I rub it. "Not my favorite topic."

Her lips thin into a line as she nods. "I can respect that." She tips her head and those silver eyes cut through all my bullshit. "I know the shit I've been through is probably nothing compared to what you've seen, but it's still enough to give me nightmares."

I don't know whether it's just Lilah, or the idea of actually talking about things I've never thought I'd be able to, but my heart is galloping in my chest. "You train for months, drills and simulations. They tell you you're ready and they send you off. They don't tell you how loud it is. When you're in the middle of a firefight..." I shake my head. "They don't tell you that you'll never hear your brother's scream over the shells. That the only way you'll know he's dead is when you turn around and see his mangled body, bleeding out into the sand."

I take a breath and hold it, waiting for the roll of acid up my throat to settle.

"They don't tell you you'll hear those shells for the rest of your life, and every time you close your eyes, you'll see it again...try to change it, put yourself where your buddy was. They don't tell you that's the only time you'll hear the scream, because it's yours, waking you from the nightmare." I swallow and glance at her. "They don't tell you shit."

She doesn't say anything, but those eyes stay fixed on mine until I turn back to the road. Her hand slides like silk over the back of mine, on the gearshift, and she threads her fingers between mine. I know she feels me shaking, but I can't stop it.

We stay just like that as I navigate us over the Grape Vine and down into the L.A. basin. When I have my shit mostly back together, I look at her. "I know you've been through some shit too. You've got the look."

"What look?"

"The 'don't mess with me' look. It's the armor everyone who's been through shit they're not really dealing with wears to keep people from noticing."

She takes her hand off mine and I wish I kept my mouth shut, but it's too late now. Can of worms opened.

"I told you my shit," she says without looking at me. "Tweaker parents."

I cut her a glance. "But there's more to it."

She stiffens, her hands pressing into the seat next to her legs. "Why would you think that?"

My eyes brush over her and I flick my T-shirt. "Matching armor."

She rolls her head toward the passenger window and watches the cars we pass for a good while. "The day of the fire, Lo and I got expelled for gambling at school. She kept all her odds spreadsheets in the school's cloud account and she'd log bets in the computer lab at lunch. Our house was always full of squatters, but when I got home early, there was only Dad and a guy I didn't know. Don't even know what happened to him after. Guess he took off or whatever. I went upstairs and the next thing I know there's screaming and…" She takes a deep breath. "I remember getting trapped on the stairs because the fire had already spread. Destiny soaked some blankets and we wrapped them around ourselves and ran through it. The fire trucks were just showing up, but Destiny and I just kept walking after we got out." She shakes her head. "It's all a little fuzzy, but I think we stayed at Lo's group home that night. After, we kicked around between some of Destiny's friends apartments until we found our crappy apartment in the Tenderloin."

She's quiet for a minute, but I wait to see if there's more. "No one ever came looking for you?" I finally ask. "CPS or the cops?"

"Destiny thought if we kept our heads down, no one would think to look for us." She shrugs. "Turns out she was right."

"Wow. So you guys have been on your own since you were fourteen?"

She turns to me then, her eyes wide, and again, I see that vulnerability. She opens her mouth and looks like she's going to say something, but then closes it again.

Acid burns through my insides at the knowledge that her drug addicted parents nearly killed both of their kids. I scrub a hand over my chin to keep from punching something. For a long time we're quiet as I get my temper under control.

"Where was the rest of your family?" I finally ask when I can keep the shake of my rage out of my voice. "Grandparents, aunts, uncles. If your parents were strung out, someone else should have stepped up and looked out for you."

"My uncle's the one who started my parents using. Grandma knew things were bad, which is why she took us in the summers, but it didn't get *really* bad until after she was in the nursing home."

"Have you seen your parents since?" I ask, fury running like a river through my words. "Confronted them?"

She shakes her head. "What's the point? It won't change anything that happened."

My jaw is clamped so tight I don't know how I'm not cracking teeth. We get stuck in some traffic getting across L.A. to the Sony Studios in Culver City. A few blocks from the parking garage, there's a diner. I pull into the lot.

Lilah makes no move to get out. "I'm not hungry."

"Me either, but you should eat something."

She shoulders open her door and gets out. I meet her at the front of the car and we head inside. We're seated at the window and she stares out at nothing as the waitress fills our coffee mugs.

"Listen, you're right about the past," I say once she's gone with our orders—a side of bacon for her and a slice of apple pie a la mode for me. "There's nothing we can do to change it. This is about right now, and right now, your best friend is about to make something pretty spectacular happen, so that's where your head should be."

She pulls her gaze back into the room and finds mine. "You're right. Fuck the past. The future's going to be kickass and I'm not going to miss it because I'm too busy wallowing over my fucked-in-the-head parents."

I nod. "That sounds about right."

We jump through all the hoops to get parked and through security, and we're led to seats in the second row, in the "family box." The minute we walk in, Lilah's face lights. Her eyes scan the room, over the stage that's being prepped and the seats where the judges or coaches or whatever sit, and she drinks it all in.

We settle into our seats and she reaches for my hand, nearly crushing it in her surprisingly strong grip. I focus on the feel of her skin on mine and realize, if I close my eyes and soften my hand, I can feel her pulse. It's racing and she's flushed with anticipation.

God, she's beautiful.

And when she smiles at me, it knocks the wind out of me.

Finally, the four coaches take their seats and the show starts.

Some spit-and-polished guy with hair as shiny as his shoes stands up onstage in a monkey suit and tells us this is what the entire season has been leading up to; that one of the final four will be crowned The Voice and score a recording contract that will launch his or her career. But all I see is Lilah. I can't take my eyes off her.

Each of the singers takes their turn, and when Shiloh is announced to perform last, Lilah screams and bounds to her feet.

I listen to Shiloh and she's good, but the honest to fuck truth is, Shiloh has nothing on Lilah.

There's a commercial break and the house lights come up. People all around us start chattering, but Lilah is still absorbing. She reaches for my hand again when they start cueing us to quiet down and the house lights lower.

The spotlight flashes to Spit and Polish, who says, "Here to sing her original song, 'More Than Nothing,' written by her best friend, Delilah Morgan, put your hands together for Shiloh Luck!"

I spin on Lilah as everyone rises to their feet and claps. She's standing next to me with her hands pressed to her flushed cheeks, an overwhelmed kid at Christmas. "Did you know?"

She nods, and there's a mix of terror and exhilaration in her eyes that makes them glow in the dim lighting. "She called me when they were deciding on songs and asked if I had anything fresh. I sent her the one I wrote for you and they loved it. I had to sign a release so they could use it."

I smile and shake my head as her friend launches into the song I first heard Lilah sing from her perch on my barstool weeks ago. As I listen, I realize the song is about so much more than I first believed. It's about breaking chains and not being afraid to live. It's about making life count. And fuck me, that's what this girl has done to me. All my fears about dying before I've lived, and missing out on something great—she's the fix to all of it. Out of the blue, she showed up in my life and made it into more than the nothing it was before. She's the thing I look forward to every morning. She's the thing that gives my life color and flavor and amperage. She brings me to life.

I can't stop staring at her as she jumps to the rhythm and sings along, oblivious to the furtive looks from people around us. And her voice does to me what it always does, wakes up the starving beast inside.

She speaks to me on every level, body, mind, and soul, and right now, they're all in agreement.

Delilah Morgan owns me.

CHAPTER 20

Lilah

Lo is crushing it and everyone is on their feet. One second I'm rocking out and the next, the fat guy to my left bounces right into me. I go flying and I find myself in Bran's arms. Pressed against his chest. His biceps ripple as his hands lock over my hips. He pulls me against him so we each have a knee between the other's, and his gaze melts me as he starts so sway to the rhythm.

All of a sudden, I'm standing five inches from the sun. I feel every hard ridge of Bran's ripped body pressed against me. I feel his hands glide to my ass and pull me tighter against his leg. And *god*, that leg. It's steel between my thighs, rubbing on my most sensitive spot and forcing my breath to catch. I close my eyes and feel my breathing go ragged. And when my lips part in a gasp that's swallowed by the pound of the music and the roar of the crowd as they woot for my best friend, Bran takes the invitation. His mouth closes over mine, insistent and unyielding, taking what he needs from me. And I give him that and more.

Our first kiss rocked my world. Our second knocked it off its axis. This one is going to blow it apart.

I claw at him, because there's suddenly no way I can get close enough. His mouth on mine goes from desperate to ravenous and he grasps my ass harder. I grind myself against his leg and drop my head back and gasp again, louder this time, as I feel my world coming apart all around me.

He knows just how to play me and I realize I'm going to come right here in the middle of a crowded television studio with my best friend tearing the place down.

The song ends and the place erupts in applause, but I barely notice because I'm crying out for an entirely different reason. It occurs to me I'm going to hate myself in just about five minutes when I realize A) I missed most of Lo's performance and B) All I care about right this second is fucking my sister's...boyfriend? Or is he just a prospect? She told me she doesn't love him. But she thinks she needs to provide me with stability, and Bran is her plan to do that.

All I know is that every time I catch him watching me play at the bar, despite my heart beating a little faster, I feel lightheaded. I can't concentrate and my fingers sometimes forget what they're supposed to be doing on the strings. I'll blank on the lyrics to a song I've sung a thousand times.

I wrote the song Shiloh just sung because he made me feel like everything wasn't shit. Looking forward to seeing him is what made my life "More than Nothing."

He messes with my head and twists my body into knots. He makes me feel electric with the slightest touch. I don't know if that's love, but I *do* know no one's ever done those things to me before.

And sure as hell, no one's ever made me come with their thigh pressed between my legs. But as I gasp out his name, sparks flash behind my closed eyelids.

The applause dies down and Bran lowers my Jell-O body into my seat as everyone begins to sit. When I glance at the guy on my other side, he's grinning at me.

The coaches are commenting on Lo's performance and I try to focus. Adam jabs at Blake that he can't win them all and they agree that that song will make Lo tough to beat.

Bran lifts my hand from where it rests on my thigh and the press of warm, rough skin against mine as he folds my hand into his sends a flood of heat through me.

I like Bran way more than I should...for a lot of reasons. I have to tell him the truth.

The rest of the show passes in a blur and I'm so wound up that I don't even realize my phone is buzzing as we navigate the crush of bodies out of the studio. I pull it from my pocket, expecting Destiny, but it's Lo.

I yank Bran to the side and answer. "Oh my god, Lo! You crushed it!"

"Because of you!" she squeals. "Did you hear Blake and Adam? They loved your song!"

"Do you have time? Can I see you?"

"No, Li. We're in the car on the way to the hotel already. But you have to stay for the results tomorrow. I need you here either way. There are tickets with your name on them at Will Call."

I cringe and look at Bran. "I got a ride from a friend, Lo. I can't stay."

Bran squints a question at me and mouths, "She wants you to stay?"

I nod.

"Then we'll stay," he says.

My heart beats out of rhythm at the thought of staying overnight in L.A. with Bran. Lo's voice draws me back to the phone. "Li? You still there?"

"My ride is okay with staying, but I have to check in with Destiny."

"Thank you!" she screeches. "I've got to go, but I'll text you tomorrow with all the details."

On the way to the parking structure, I call Destiny and she says she's fine with me staying as long as Bran's looking after me. When we reach his car, the anticipation is choking me. It never occurred to me that we'd be staying in L.A. overnight. If Bran gets a room, my choices are to share it with him or sleep alone in his car. It's clear from the way I ache low in my belly remembering what he just did to me in the studio, that if my body got a vote, I'd be sleeping in Bran's bed tonight.

But I can't do that to my sister.

He clicks the lock. "How do you want to play this?"

I look at him and realize he's thinking about the logistics too. But his smoldering gaze leaves little doubt what he hopes my answer will be. "I can't afford a room."

"I've got it covered," he says, sliding into the car.

I lower myself into his passenger seat. "I didn't bring fresh clothes for tomorrow."

"So you want to head home?"

I think about that and my heart turns to stone. I can't leave when Lo is so close. "No."

Without another word, he pulls out of the garage and heads back the way we came, toward the highway. We're quiet as he drives. I don't know about him, but I'm too nervous to talk without my voice cracking. All I can think about is what's going to happen when this car stops and Bran gets me alone in a hotel room. He passes a few nicer looking hotels and pulls into a small parking lot in front of a two-story building near the entrance ramp to the highway. There's a big neon sign on top that says MOTEL. Under it is a smaller lit half moon.

We take the last parking spot and walk into the motel office.

"You got a room available?" Bran asks as he approaches the desk.

The guy nods. "One left." He glances at me, then back at Bran. "It's a king."

"What's the rate?" Bran asks, fishing his wallet out of his back pocket.

"One thirty plus tax."

Bran nods and flips a card out of his wallet. "One night."

The clerk gets us checked in and hands Bran two keycards. Bran lays his hand on the small of my back and guides me out the door and toward the stairs up from the parking lot to the second floor. He slides the card through the lock and opens the door onto a room that looks clean enough, but what holds my attention is the big king size bed taking up most of the space.

He steps through and closes the door, and the next second I'm wrapped in his arms. He hasn't forgotten where we left off at the studio, apparently, because his kiss is demanding and leaves no doubt where this is headed. And when my T-shirt passes over my head, my theory is confirmed. Just behind it, my bra hits the floor. And then he's got my jeans undone and over my hips before I even have time to think.

So I don't. I just go with the sensations that are sweeping over me and pulling me under.

I kick my jeans off and Bran lowers me onto the bed. He's still fully dressed and there's something totally hot about him holding that power over me. His mouth starts a slow exploration of my neck and shoulders, then his lips circle my breast before his tongue glides over the nipple, pricking it into a hard nub. When he blows gently on the wet tip it sends a rush skittering over my skin and I press my head back and arch against his mouth, needing it on me again.

He finds my other nipple and his teeth graze over it, sending shockwaves through me straight to my groin. My body must be an open book, because as he slides up and kisses my mouth again, slow and deep, one hand glides down my hip and comes to rest over my panties, cupping me. His fingers press between my legs as he grinds his palm against my clit. I gasp and arch up again.

"You're so fucking wet," he groans against my mouth.

"I want you," I say, my voice so thick with need and desire I barely recognize it.

He draws back and examines my face with hooded eyes. "You tell me that and I'm not going to stop, Lilah. I've wanted to fuck you since the moment I laid eyes on you."

I lay my arms to the side and spread my legs, opening myself up to him fully. "Then fuck me."

A devilishly heart-stopping half smile curves his mouth before it's on mine again. He kisses down my body, his hands and mouth stopping briefly to pay homage to my breasts, before moving lower. He drags the tip of his tongue along the waistband of my underwear, then seals his mouth over my clit, sucking me through the thin cotton. It's only a minute before he has me clawing at the sheets and crying out, so close to coming. But before I do, he kneels between my legs and looks down at me like a wolf at his fresh kill. He divests me of my last shred of clothing, then takes each of my feet and rests the arches on his shoulders, opening my knees. I am totally on display for him and if I was wet before, I'm gushing now.

He slicks a finger over my clit, then sinks it deep inside me and twists. The next stroke, another finger joins it, and God, he knows what he's doing. With just his touch, I feel on the edge of exploding. My hips start moving to his rhythm and his gaze becomes fierce and animal as he watches his fingers fuck me. But again, just when he has me on the edge of coming, he stops and trails his wet fingertips down the inside of my thigh. That devil's smile paints his face again as he slips them into his mouth and sucks my juices off of them.

I close my eyes as every muscle south of my waist contracts hard.

"You like that?" he asks, his voice the growl of the wolf he's become.

"Yes," I say, opening my eyes and finding his.

He slips his shirt over his head and all his cut, tattooed glory is right there in front of me—a masterpiece I never expected to be able to touch. He flicks open the button of his jeans and when he pushes them down his hips, along with his boxers, his enormous erection springs free, like a beast uncaged.

I trail my toes down his torso and glide them along his hard length. His eyes widen in surprise and he holds his breath and moves his hips to my rhythm when I start to toe fuck him.

But then he growls and the next second all of his two hundred and thirty pounds are on top of me. I'm so wet that he glides right into me without any resistance, despite the fact that he's stretching me nearly to pain. I grab his ass and spread wide as he rams into me, over and over, each thrust accompanied by a grunt or a growl. We've become pure animal, pure instinct, needing only the physical. I'm crying out, not words but primal sounds I didn't even know I was capable of. I rock my hips against him with each thrust, harder and deeper than the one before. It's only a few minutes later that I topple over the edge and come harder than I ever have, mewling loudly with my release. He gives one last thrust and then pulls out, coming a river across my stomach.

I don't know what I was doing with Tyrell, but it sure as hell wasn't this.

He gives an intense whole-body shudder before dropping onto his back next to me, panting. "Fuck me," he groans. "I've never come that fast in my life."

"I inspire you."

He stares at the ceiling and shakes his head. "You sure as hell do *something* to me." His gaze turns to mine. "And just so you know, next time I'm going to take my time and make you come so many times you lose count."

The swollen lips between my legs throb with the thought that there's going to be a "next time." And on the heels of that thought is Destiny. She's working her ass off for me while I'm fucking the man she wants. A man who's fucked her too.

Ants crawl under my skin and I push up from the bed and lock the bathroom door. I clean myself off then sit on the toilet with my elbows on my knees and my head in my hands.

What am I doing? There are so many reasons why what I just did was wrong. Destiny is only one of them.

I needed to tell Bran the truth before things went too far.

But here we are, too far. And it's too late.

CHAPTER 21

Bran

For the first time in my life, I don't mind not sleeping. I lay in bed and listen to Lilah breathe. When she first came back from the bathroom, she was a little distant, and I was afraid I'd hurt her. But then I realized.

Destiny.

She's feeling guilty, and I guess that shouldn't be a surprise. I give her some space and she curls onto her side with her back to me. But it's only a few minutes before she rolls to face me.

She reaches for me and trails a finger along the grooves of my pecs. "I don't know what I'm doing. In my head, I know we shouldn't have done that, but I want to do it again."

That's all I have to hear. I pull her on top of me and before she ever touches me, I'm hard as stone. She lifts her hips and sinks slowly down my length, and she's so wet and so fucking tight that I'm afraid of breaking my promise to make this one last.

She leans down so those spectacular tits press against my chest and whispers, "I'm on the pill."

I sink my fingers into her hips and thrust hard into her. She gasps and buries her face in my neck. I pump to her rhythm as she grinds against me, taking special care to make sure I hit her clit with each thrust. Her breathing gets ragged and her cries become more feral, and when she comes a few minutes later, she bites down hard on my shoulder.

I flip her onto her back before she's even done screaming and go down on her, sucking her swollen clit hard into my mouth. When I graze it with my teeth, she screams again, and then again when I swirl the tip of my tongue over it and suck. Her hands grab my head and she grinds hard against my face, and her cum is like honey on my tongue.

Once I've lapped it all up, I kneel between her legs and drape her knees over my thighs. She's every fucking thing I knew she'd be, and together, we're fireworks. I give her a minute to catch her breath before my fingers and mouth start a full exploration. I want to know what every inch of her body tastes like.

By the time I roll her on her stomach and sink my steel cock balls deep inside her, she's come twice more. I pump hard into her, my hand playing her clit until she's screaming again. And when I feel her convulse under me, I thrust deep and unload into her.

I collapse onto the bed next to her, breathing hard. It's minutes later that I have my breath back, and I realize I'm half asleep when I hear a whispered, "I love you," so blurry and muffled in the pillow that I could have imagined it.

Because, Christ, I want to hear it.

She doesn't move again, and I listen as her breathing slows. Her smell, warm vanilla, is on my skin. The taste of her nectar is still in my mouth. She's long and lean and tanned, her platinum hair fanned over the pillow and half covers her face where she passed out facedown after I ravaged her. The inferno of our sex is evidenced in the pink of her skin and the twist of the sheets around my torso and legs.

This is the perfect moment.

I close my eyes and just live in it for as long as I can.

An agonized cry rips through the still of the room and I bolt out of bed, instantly looking through the faint pink of the morning light through the open curtains for the threat. It takes me a second to get my bearings, and when I do, I realize for the first time in years, it was Lilah's nightmare that woke me instead of my own.

She's panting and her hair is stuck to her face with sweat, but she's not fully awake.

I brush her hair back. "Lilah?"

She moans, the sound of a wounded animal, then cries out and bolts to a sitting position, nearly knocking heads with me. She looks at me with frightened, unfocused eyes and shoves me back. "No!"

"Lilah," I say again, keeping my voice low. "It's me, Bran."

Her eyes finally seem to focus. "Bran?"

I pull her to my chest. "You're okay. Everything's okay." I know they're meaningless words, but I also know firsthand there's nothing I can really do to dispel her demons. They leave when they're good and ready.

I lay back and bring her with me. Her head is on my chest and I stroke her hair as she slowly comes down from the nightmare.

"If you ever need to talk about it…" I say, but leave the thought there for her to pick up if she wants.

She doesn't, and I'm not offended. I'd never presume to push her to relive her nightmare and think that's really going to help. We all have things that are better kept locked away in the pits of our souls.

Just when I think she's falling asleep again, she lifts her head and kisses the scruff under my jaw. "I don't want to go back to sleep."

I pull her closer and kiss her, and her hand finds my flaccid cock. She strokes and only a few seconds later, I'm hard and ready.

I flip us and pin her under me, then sink myself into her. "Did you say what I think you said last night?"

She looks up at me, all sex and desire. "That depends on what you think I said."

I pump slowly, feeling her along my entire length. I can't stop the shudder when her fingertips glide over my back and settle on my ass.

I seat myself fully inside her and stop. "Say it again."

Her eyes flash. "What?"

I start moving, deeper, but still agonizingly slowly. She responds by arching into me and digging her fingers into my flesh.

I pull her hands off my ass and lock my fingers through hers, pinning the backs of her hands to the mattress on either side of her head. "Say it."

A wicked smile teases the corners of her mouth. "I don't know what you're talking about."

I thrust harder and she rocks against me, closes her eyes and moans. I seal my mouth over hers to capture the sound of her lust. Her legs part wider, giving me everything, and her heels dig into my ass, pulling me deeper.

I fuck her slowly and thoroughly, and when she's right on the edge of falling to pieces under me, I stop. "Say it."

"No!" she cries, thrusting her hips upward against mine and grinding. "God, no," she pants. "Don't stop."

I let go of her hands and hold her face, forcing her to see me. "Say what you said last night."

Her eyes flash white fire into mine. "I love you."

I smile and glide my hands between the mattress and her ass, lifting her. I fuck her hard and deep, giving her everything I have, and when she comes a moment later, I let go and come with her.

I collapse on top of her. "Good," I breathe in her ear. "Then I'm not in this alone."

As we catch our breath, her stomach growls and I realize I haven't fed her since lunch yesterday. I roll off her and grab my jeans from the floor. I look back from the door at her glowing, ravaged body. "Don't move. I'll be back."

She gives me a sultry smirk as I shut the door. I jog half a block to the Starbucks I saw last night on the way in and I grab some coffees and a bag of pastries. When I come back, Lilah's in the shower.

And, fuck me, just thinking about her in there has me hard again.

I down half my coffee and bring hers with me into the bathroom, where I shuck my jeans onto the floor. I pull back the curtain and she's wet and shimmering. A fucking goddess.

I fix her in my gaze. "I told you not to move."

"And you think I'm just going to do what you say?" One eyebrow raises in a challenge. "Have you met me?"

A wave of pure elation forces a laugh rumbling up my throat. Fuck, that feels good, like shaking all the sludge in my soul loose. It has to be high school, the last time I felt this unburdened.

"Coffee?" I ask, holding up her cup.

She steps out of the water and her eyes skate over me as she takes it from my hand. They stop on my raging boner. "How many times can you go?"

I blow out a laugh. "Apparently, when it comes to you, there's no limit."

I step into the shower and watch her long throat move as she takes a swallow of her coffee. She hands it back to me and I take a drink before setting it on the counter. I close the curtain and she pulls me into the water, against her slick body. She loops her arms around my neck and spreads her knees over my hips when I lift her by the ass and lower her onto my stiff cock.

"How many times have you gone before?" she asks, grinding her hips and driving me fucking nuts.

I pull my face out of her neck and look at her. "You really want to talk about this?"

She nods. "What's your record?"

I turn us and press her back against the tile, driving myself into her. "We've already shattered that."

"So less than four," she muses.

"One," I say with my next thrust. "Or maybe two, but that was back in high school."

She draws back and looks me in the eyes. "Why only once?"

I fight to hold her gaze. She deserves to know what I am. Or was...until I found her. "With the others, it was just a fuck. Once it was over, I was over them. They left, I usually never saw them again, end of story."

She nods and grinds her hips against mine. "How many girls?"

"Christ, Lilah. You really want to do this now?"

She grips my shoulders tighter and rides me to the tip and back down to the root, grinding hard against me. "I can't think of anytime better. How many?"

When my cock pulses inside her, I realize having this conversation balls deep inside her is kind of hot. "Maybe a hundred."

"That's a lot," she says, bracing her back against the tile for leverage and pumping harder.

"What about you? How many?"

"One."

I thrust deep. "Four's a record for you too, then."

"I meant one guy." She kisses me. "Two now." I know my shock is plain on my face when she laughs. "Sorry if I didn't have an endless stream of barflies to keep me company."

I start fucking her in earnest, hard and deep. "It wasn't company I was looking for. It was a distraction."

She stops moving and looks at me. "From the nightmares."

I nod.

She kisses me again and our mouths stay locked as we give into every base desire we feel for each other. I'm so deep inside her I feel like I'm taking root somewhere in her soul, and with each desperate thrust, she's climbing a little deeper into mine.

After we come, she tips her head back against the tile and breathes, "Why am I any different?"

I wrap her so tightly in my arms I nearly crush her. "Because you're the one who made them go away."

Lilah's sweaty palm is pressed against mine as the show comes back from commercial and the stage lights flash. The suspense music cues and Spit and Polish says it's time to find out which of our four finalists is The Voice. Shiloh and the three others stand in the spotlights, trying to look like they're not flipping out. He announces fourth place, then third. Neither are Shiloh.

With each name, Lilah's grip tightens. When I look at her, she's stone, not even blinking, but I can feel her tremor.

"And then there were two," Spit and Polish says, exaggeratedly slowly, dragging out every syllable. "Essie Franklin, Shiloh Luck, one of you *is* The Voice." He pauses a moment while the cheers drown out the dramatic background music. "It's time to find out who it is!" He backs away, giving center stage to the contestants. "The winner of The Voice is…"

One second.

Two.

Three.

Four.

Five.

"Oh, God," Lilah whimpers from beside me. I glance at her and her head is bowed, her eyes pressed tightly shut.

"Shiloh Luck!" Spit and Polish bellows.

As the building erupts in applause, Lilah's legs collapse and she drops into chair, her face in her hands.

I lower myself to my seat and pull her into my arms. "Congrats."

She yanks her head up, panic filling her eyes. "It's my song."

"That's good, right?"

She nods and stands, staring at her friend as Spit and Polish babbles some nonsense over the roar of the crowd. "It's awesome...and scary."

I pull her to my shoulder again and she shakes in my arms. Spit and Polish is still talking, and I catch a few words. "Two seasons in a row....sixteen-year-old winners...youngest ever..."

As his words sink through my consciousness and I really hear them, that warning buzz starts under my skin...the same one I felt every time I was in the field in Afghanistan. My internal alarm system. I peel Lilah off me and look at her face, tears caught in the corners of those silver eyes.

"Shiloh's sixteen?" I ask, the buzz turning to the crackle of an electric fence.

The shocked elation on her face drops instantly into dread, and her panicked eyes widen. "I wanted to tell you...I meant to, but..." She trails off with a cringe.

"*You're* sixteen..." I say, my lungs constricting so hard almost no sound comes out.

When I get no answer except an apologetic squint, I drop into my seat and scrub a hand over my face. I just spent all night fucking a sixteen-year-old's brains out. "Jesus Christ."

"Bran..." she says, lowering herself into her seat. "It doesn't matter, right? It's just a number."

I rip my head out of my hand and glare at her. "A number that will get me fucking *arrested*!"

The crowd is still going wild for the new Voice. I hardly notice them.

"Do you have any idea how old I am, Lilah?" I growl, the animal inside ripping free of its restraints, freeing the rage I've fought so hard to keep buried. "I'm twenty-fucking-six."

She swallows and more tears leak over her lashes.

As Shiloh launches into the song Lilah wrote, I notice people are shooting us glances. This is my worst fucking nightmare—a crowded set full of people witnessing my undoing.

I stand and yank Lilah up by the wrist. "We're going."

She doesn't resist as I drag her up the aisle and out the back doors. I let her go once we're away from the sea of bodies and storm to my car, barely caring if she's following.

"You said you were twins," I spit when we reach the Torino and I find her behind me.

She shakes her head and there's fight in her expression now. She's nearly as pissed as me, but she has no right to be. "*You* said we were twins."

"But you didn't correct me," I say, nearly yanking my door off the hinges.

She shrugs. "We were flirting. I didn't think it mattered how old I was."

"And last night, when we were fucking?" I yell over the roof of the car. "You didn't think it mattered then either?"

She pulls open her door and slides in without answering.

I drop into my seat and tear out of the garage. We're on the highway before she speaks again. "No one's ever looked at me the way you do. I've never felt how you make me feel." She pauses, swallows then takes a deep breath. "I started to tell you the other night at the bar...but then I couldn't because..." She tips her head back and stares at the roof. "I was in love with you and...I didn't want you to quit looking at me like that."

"And you thought I'd still look at you that way through my *prison bars*?" I slam my palm against the steering wheel. "Fuck, Lilah! I have two friends who have been arrested for doing what we did. One of them spent two months in jail."

There's no response except for soft sniffling, but I refuse to look at her. Miles later, when I finally do, things happen inside me that can't happen anymore. I can't want this girl. This *baby*. I can't be in love with her.

Her phone buzzes and I hear her blow out a shaky sigh before lifting it to her ear. "Hey, Destiny. We're on our way."

I hear Destiny screaming excitedly through the phone about Shiloh.

"Yeah, it was amazing," Lilah says, but there's no enthusiasm behind it.

Destiny says something else, low enough now that I don't pick up anything but my name. "Yes, he kept his eye on me."

My eyes, my mouth, my hands, my cock. I kept a lot of things on her.

She waits through Destiny's response. "Yeah. He's been great, Destiny. We'll be home in a few hours." She hangs up and lowers her hand. "She thinks you're a great guy."

I give my head a small shake, my jaw so tight my teeth ache.

"She wanted me to talk her up while we drove, make you see how awesome she is." She blows out a bitter laugh. "Instead, I opened my legs for you. That's the kind of person I am—the kind that stabs her sister in the back. Destiny's the good one. You should have stuck with her."

"You should have told me the truth," I grind out.

I keep one fist tight on the gearshift and the other on the steering wheel, because if I don't I can't guarantee they won't end up around her neck. Or in her hair. Or ripping her clothes off her fucking incredible body.

Because, despite everything, I know I never could have settled for Destiny.

Not when there's Lilah.

CHAPTER 22

Lilah

Jon honks out front and I grab my messenger bag and head down the stairs. When I slide into his car, he wiggles his eyebrows.

"You fucking slut," he says, his mouth pulling into that puppy grin.

I know what this is about. Apparently, the cameras cut to me during Lo's original song Tuesday night and caught me kissing Bran. Jon texted me on our way home last night to congratulate me on Lo's win and to tell me that, as my boyfriend, he was sorely disappointed in me for cheating on him. But he put one of those winking emoticons after the message. Plus, Jon's always totally full of shit, so I wasn't really worried. About him, anyway.

But I was terrified Destiny'd seen it.

She hadn't sounded upset when she'd called, but I couldn't imagine that she hadn't watched the show, so I braced myself when Bran dropped me off at the apartment at one thirty this morning.

She was just home from the bar and she threw her arms around me and jumped up and down at Lo's win. But nothing about kissing Bran. She said Sam Hill had been unusually busy for a Tuesday night and she hadn't caught the whole semi-finals show, but she'd been able to watch most of the results last night.

I'm so excited for Lo, but everything with Bran feels like the end of my world. I tried to seem as ecstatic as I should be when I told Destiny how awesome the trip was, but I wasn't feeling it and she could tell. When she asked if I was okay, I told her I was tired and asked if I could skip school today. Her answer was an emphatic no. Thankfully, she was too busy playing mother hen to ask too many more questions about the trip.

So, bullet dodged.

"He looked hot," Jon says, watching me expectantly. "Who was he?"

"Just a friend."

"Ha!" he says, slapping his hand against the steering wheel. "Well, as your friend, I'm filing a formal complaint that I have yet to receive my tonsil exam. You seem very thorough."

I shove his shoulder. "Shut up and drive."

He peals away from the curb and we wind our way up the hill toward school.

"You should know it was all over Instagram," he says as he drives. "Everyone's talking about you."

My eyes fly wide and cut to him. "What?"

"There were a lot of people from school watching, I guess." His voice lowers and becomes more serious than I've ever heard it. "Someone snapped a screenshot of you kissing that guy and tagged me, because, you know, I'm your boyfriend. It sort of went viral and pretty much everyone at school's reposted."

I hang my head. "Fuck."

"I just thought you should know why everyone's going to be staring at you as soon as we walk in."

"Is it going to make things hard for you?" I ask, focusing on that part of this nightmare instead of the part that could get Bran thrown in jail.

He shrugs and tries for a cocky grin. "Not after I break up with you very loudly and publicly at your locker in about five minutes. There'll probably be pics on Instagram before first period starts, so I'll be vindicated. I'll be the ex of the girl whose bestie just won *The Voice*." He flicks a wrist at himself. "Instant chick magnet."

I turn in my seat to look at him. "Okay…so where exactly are we in this whole girls versus boys thing?"

"I'm thinking about opting for both," he says with a shrug. "Why miss out on half the fun?"

I pick his hand off his thigh and hold it between mine as we pull into the lot. "Just be careful. I don't want to see you get hurt."

He rolls into a space and cuts the engine, then leans over and kisses my forehead. "Too late. My first girlfriend has already crushed my heart."

❖

Everything at school went pretty much how Jon predicted. I go straight to my job at the market after school and the manager, Gillian, puts me to work restocking the cereal shelves. There was apparently a run on Lucky Charms this morning, so I go to the stockroom to find the case then head back to the shelves.

It's mindless work, and I let myself drift. Where I land is face up on the bed at the Half Moon Motel, Bran's solid weight between my legs, driving into me. Every nerve ending in my body catches fire with the memory. Right here in the cereal aisle, my lips tingle and my breath catches and I'm fairly certain I'm about to spontaneously combust.

I close my eyes and trail a finger down my neck, remembering the brush of Bran's lips there, the warmth of his breath feathering over my skin.

"Delilah!"

Destiny's panicked voice calling my name rips me from the fantasy just as she grips my shoulder and whips me around to face her. Her expression is a toxic blend of anger and fear when she holds up her phone for me to see. On the screen is the picture of me in the studio audience, pressed against Bran. He's got handfuls of my ass and I've got fistfuls of his hair, and we're devouring each other.

"What the hell is this?" she shrieks.

I feel my face crumble. "I'm sorry, Destiny…it just…"

I can't even finish the lie. It didn't "just happen." We'd been building up to it for weeks. If I'm totally honest with myself, I've *wanted* it to happen since that first night I walked into Sam Hill.

"You're sixteen!" she reminds me.

I shake my head. "Bran didn't know that until yesterday…after…"

Her eyes widen. "After what, Delilah? What else happened?"

I bring a hand up to my hide face. "It wasn't his fault. It was all me. If he knew, he wouldn't have—"

Her hands fly to her mouth as she cuts me off with her, "Oh my God!"

"I'm so sorry, Destiny. I know you like him."

Her jaw flexes and rage burns in her eyes. I glance over her shoulder and see a tiny Hispanic woman staring at us from the end of the cereal aisle. Past her, Gillian watches from the counter up front. I knew Destiny and I would have to have this conversation, but I was hoping we could clear the air in private.

Destiny will understand when I tell her we're in love. I just have to make her see that neither of us meant to hurt her.

But the next second, we knock into the Hispanic woman as Destiny drags me toward the door by the arm. We're halfway down the block when I realize where we're headed.

I yank out of her grasp before we make the police station door. "What are you doing, Destiny?"

"He's a pedophile. You have to file a report. If he…" Her face crumples into a deep grimace as her eyes course down my body. "There might still be evidence."

I shove away from her. "He didn't rape me!"

"If he touched you, he did," she says, her lip curling in disgust.

I shake my head and back away. "I won't report him. He didn't do anything wrong."

I take off running, and end up at Sam Hill, but as my thoughts start to untangle, I realize I can't go in there. Bran's probably not here yet anyway, and if Destiny's at the police station, I need to stay as far away from Bran as I can.

But I can't let the police get their hands on me either. Because there *is* evidence. I'm sore and bruised and I don't know how long DNA hangs around.

I keep off the beaten path and work my way up the hill to Jon's, hoping he's home from practice. When I get there, the Mustang isn't in the driveway, so I sit on a rock under a tree in the woods behind his house and hug my knees to my chest while I wait.

When he finally pulls up half an hour later, I sprint for his car and jump in the passenger side.

"Whoa," he says. "Sneak attack. Look, Lilah, I know this breakup has been hard on you, but—"

I slap a hand over his mouth to shut him up. "The guy I was kissing is twenty-six and my sister's going to have him arrested."

His eyes widen and when I don't feel his mouth trying to move under my palm, I peel my hand back. He just stares at me. For the first time ever, he doesn't have a comeback.

"I need somewhere I can lay low for a few days until Destiny calms down. Do you think your parents would let me stay here?"

He nods slowly.

"Okay." I take a deep breath to settle my jumbled nerves. "Okay."

I follow Jon inside. His brother is in front of the TV, but otherwise no one's home. We go to his room and he closes his door. I collapse onto his bed, but then realize with a jolt of adrenaline that I need to warn Bran.

I pull my phone from my pocket and dial. After a few rings, it goes to voicemail. "Destiny knows. Call me." I disconnect and resist the urge to throw my phone across the room.

He's probably not answering because he's pissed at me, but if the police show up and haul him to jail, he's going to wish he took that call.

CHAPTER 23

Bran

I climb out of my car in front of Sam Hill and see I have a welcoming committee. Destiny's standing in front of the door, her fists bunched at her sides, ready for a fight.

So it starts.

"You sick bastard," she shrieks as I approach. Her arm swings out, but I'm ready for her and catch her wrist before her palm makes my face.

I probably should have let her hit me. Fuck knows, I deserve it.

"You got tired of fucking me and moved on to my baby sister?" she spits. "I'm going to make sure everyone in this fucking town knows what a twisted creep you are." She swings her arm wildly at the front of the bar.

"Imagine posters on every storefront with your face and the caption 'baby fucker.' Think that will get people's attention?"

"Do what you have to do," I say, brushing past her.

"Tell your mother I quit," she shouts at my back. "I can't even make myself set foot inside there to do it myself. And if you ever come near me or my sister again, I'll call the cops and have your pedophile ass thrown in jail."

I push through the door, then stop and rub a hand down my face. "Fuck," I growl under my breath.

Because my sorry truth is, I can't stop thinking about Lilah. No one's ever turned me inside out the way she does. No one's ever had me thinking past the first fuck. But Lilah has flipped everything on its head.

My phone rings and I fish it from my pocket. When Lilah's number flashes on the screen, I take a breath and brace myself for everything that voice does to me. But then I realize, if I do this, hold on when I should let go, Destiny *will* follow through on her threat. Lilah will be dragged through the mud. She'll be forced to testify to every depraved thing I did to her.

I'm not going to put her through that. So I send the call to voicemail, then delete the message without listening.

CHAPTER 24

Lilah

I listen to Jon's mom's side of the conversation as she talks to Destiny. She insisted on calling after dinner to tell her I'm staying overnight. "I don't believe it's my place to get into the middle of a family dispute," Bethany says, "but that said, Lilah seems quite shaken. It might do you both good to have a night apart to pull your thoughts together so you can work out whatever the issue is with clearer minds."

I pray to God Destiny won't enlighten her on the "issue." I'm not mentally prepared to defend it in any way other to say I love Bran, and I feel like I need more to justify it. Because what Bran and I did technically *is* illegal in the state of California. I Googled it on Jon's laptop before his parents got home. I thought if I told the cops I consented, he would be okay. It turns out consent doesn't matter. I'm sixteen and it's illegal for a twenty-six-year-old to touch me with any sexual intent.

Destiny says something and Bethany's calm demeanor doesn't change, so I'm sure she didn't spill my secret. When she hangs up, she smiles. "Family is the most important thing, Lilah. I hope you take this time to truly search your soul and find a way to mend this fence."

I nod, but I'm pretty sure the fence is trampled beyond repair.

Jon and I go upstairs and sprawl across his bed with our algebra homework while Bethany makes up the double bed in the guest room.

"So...are you going to tell me what's really going on?" Jon asks from under long blond lashes. He's been uncharacteristically subdued since I told him I needed a place to stay. "Shoot me, but I checked your search history. Did you have sex with that guy?"

I tuck my legs underneath me. "Can I plead the fifth?"

"You slut!" he says with a grin, holding up a hand for a fist bump.

I shove his hand away. "Did you know the legal age of consent is sixteen in more than half of the states?"

He nods. "I saw the Wikipedia page in your history."

I flop backward onto the bed. "I know he's older but we just clicked, you know? Even though I knew it was wrong, I started feeling things that were totally out of my control."

"Such as?"

I roll on my side and prop my head in my hand. "I didn't choose to fall for him, but it was like a freight train. There was nothing I could do to stop it."

He raises his eyebrows and laughs, but it's a little bitter. "You're going to sit there and explain to *me* that you don't get to choose who you love?"

I crawl closer and pull him down with me, wrapping my arms around his neck. "I guess you get that part already."

"He goes to Redwood High, and he's a junior. Plays linebacker. I've crushed on him since we talked after our first game this season."

"The guy from the party?" I ask. "The cute one?"

He nods.

I yank the pillow out from under his head. "Then why'd you say he wasn't your type?"

He takes a deep breath and stares at the ceiling. "Do you have any idea how hard high school is for a guy? We're supposed be trying to fuck all the cheerleaders, not the opposing team."

I pull him tighter into the hug. "I love you too, if that helps."

He rolls his head and smiles that rubber smile. "Slut."

I go to my job after school, not sure if I even still have one.

"So, what was that yesterday?" Gillian asks when I walk in, her expression suspicious and her arms folded tightly across her chest.

I glance around and find the store empty, save us. "I'm sorry about the scene...and leaving," I say, evading the question. "It won't happen again."

She looks at me a moment longer. "You know I can only pay you for the hour you were here yesterday."

I nod.

She turns her back and starts straightening the cartons of cigarettes on the shelf behind the counter. "I took care of the cereal, but I need you need to check the pet food section and diapers."

"Got it." I turn for the shelves and breath a relieved sigh once I'm hidden in them. For the next five hours, I wait for the other shoe to drop…Destiny, or worse, the police to show up and make another scene. At eight when Gillian flips the open sign in the door to closed, both relief and dread wend through my insides. No public scene, but now I have to go home and face Destiny one on one.

I told her the truth. Besides Bran and I, she and Jon are the only other people on the planet who know what happened in that motel room. She's the only person who could hurt Bran.

I've stalked my phone, waiting for a text or call from Bran. So far, nothing. If he listened to the message, he knows he's in danger. I have to talk Destiny down.

I unlock the flimsy street door and trudge up the stairs. When I walk in to the apartment, I don't see Destiny, but I do see boxes stacked on the counters. I look inside and find our entire kitchen is already packed into them.

Destiny comes out of her bedroom and just looks at me. The disappointment in her eyes is glaringly apparent, but there's less unbridled fury than was there yesterday.

I hold up a hand lamely. "Hi."

"Are your thoughts straight?" she asks with a sour expression, and I realize she's mocking Bethany.

"Straighter."

She moves to the couch and drops into it. "Then explain it to me."

I lower myself into the cushions on the other end. "When I met Bran, I didn't know you were into him. I didn't know about your 'grand plan,'" I say, making air quotes with my fingers. "But the thing is, Destiny, Bran deserves more than to be your security blanket."

Her frown deepens. "This isn't about me or my plan or anything but the fact that I trusted you to his care and he took advantage of the situation. He's not right, Lilah. No normal guy his age is going to take a sixteen-year-old to bed."

I shake my head. "He didn't know."

"That's bullshit," she spits. "We talked about you. I'm sure I said something at some point. He knew."

I picture his face at the show Wednesday, the shock. No. The *horror*. He couldn't have acted that. And what would be the point of pretending? "Tell me what you think you said to him about my age."

She shoots out of the couch and throws her hands in the air. "I've worked with him for two months. You've come up more than once. There's no way he didn't know."

"You're wrong," I challenge.

She glares at me a moment longer, then grabs a box off the living room floor and turns back to the hall. "There are boxes in your room. I'm picking up the U-Haul tomorrow."

"What about the car? It's still not fixed," I say, grabbing at any straw.

"I sold it to the guy for parts," she says, like it's no big deal. But it's a huge deal. She's always said when this one died we'd never be able to afford another.

Panic kicks in my chest. This is really happening. "Where are we going?"

She spins on me. "How the fuck should I know? I just know we can't stay here."

She disappears into her room and I drop back onto the couch. It's not like Destiny to be so impulsive. She's the duck person. They all need to be in a row before she makes a decision. Even when we left San Francisco a few months ago, she had this apartment and the job lead at Sam Hill before we got here.

And now she doesn't even know where we're going.

I pull my phone out and text Jon. *We're leaving.* Then I pull up Bran's number and stare at it for a long time before typing in three short words and hitting send.

He may not want to hear them, but if I'm never going to see him again, he needs to know.

CHAPTER 25

Bran

Told Ma I was sick and stayed home tonight. And I *am* sick. In the head.

It's after midnight and I can't stop staring at Lilah's text. I sit on the couch with a pot of black coffee and recite the Gettysburg Address over and over, hoping it will take my mind off her. She's six-fucking-teen. I have T-shirts older than her. I lost my virginity when she was five. But even as I recite, my eyes course over the text.

I love you.

Fuck.

I coerced her into saying it right out loud to my face on Wednesday morning, and when I heard it coming from her mouth, my heart burst open at the seams, just like the fucking Grinch. She's changed me fundamentally, like a shift of magnetic poles, and I can't even remember how to be who I was before.

I think about the lyrics of the song she wrote, how she kissed me as Shiloh sang her words.

"Fuck!" I growl, shoving up from the couch.

I pace the window like a caged beast, staring toward town, in the direction I know she is. My heart's at a wild gallop and my breathing's short. I'm too fucking young to be having a heart attack, but that's how it feels. In the chaos of my thoughts, only one is clear. Lilah's my addiction and I can't quit her. I can't give her up without a fight.

There's only one person who can hurt us. One person to fight.

I yank on my jeans and grab a hoodie on my way out the door, then take off at a jog to my carport as tug it on. I burn rubber and am across town in a heartbeat.

The streets of downtown are deserted. It's after one, so even Sam Hill is locked up. It's so quiet that when I bang on Lilah's door, it sounds like shots in the night.

I look up at the dark second story windows and after a few second, one of them lights. When it lifts, I'm hoping for Lilah, but it's Destiny's scowl that meets my gaze. "I'm calling the cops!" she yells.

I hold up my hands in surrender. "I just want to talk."

Daggers rain down on me from her glare. "Stay away from us."

I bang on the door again out of sheer desperation. "Lilah!"

Destiny's gone from the window the next second and I hear yelling. I spin for the door and one good kick with my biker boot blows it right off the hinges, just like I knew it would. I bound up the stairs, two at a time, and pound on the door at the top.

"Get out of the way, Destiny!" I hear Lilah shout.

"Lilah!" I call as I rattle the knob.

This door's a little sturdier, but I could get through it if I had to. I ram my shoulder into it and hear the splinter of wood near the deadbolt. But just as I'm regrouping for my next assault, it swings open and Lilah is standing there. Behind her, boxes are stacked on the counters and small kitchen table.

"What's going on?" I ask.

Destiny yanks her sister back by an arm. "We're getting the hell out of here before you can do any more damage."

I step closer. "To who, Destiny?"

She backs away from me, her sister in her grasp. "Lilah is *sixteen*! She's my responsibility. I trusted you to watch after her, and instead, you raped her!"

"Stop!" Lilah says, shoving away from Destiny. "I love him. He didn't rape me."

Destiny spins on her sister. "That's not what the cops or the courts will say. You're too young to get it, Lilah, but he's sick."

Tears well in Lilah's eye as she shakes her head. "He didn't know."

"He made you believe that because he's twisted. He wanted to fuck you so lulled you into a false sense of security." Destiny's glare nearly cuts me in half when her eyes find me. "He doesn't care about anyone but himself. He uses and takes what he wants, and when he's done he tosses his victims aside like so much trash."

"You weren't a victim," I say, lifting a hand. "I never forced you to do anything."

Her face is so twisted with hate it's barely recognizable. "You are a vile, stinking pile of filth, and I will see you rot in jail."

"Are you really protecting your sister, Destiny? Or are you just getting revenge on me?" I stare her down. "Hate me all you want for falling in love with your sister instead of you, but don't drag her through this."

"He never—" Lilah starts, reaching for Destiny's arm.

Whatever she was going to say is cut short when Destiny spins on her and swings, taking her to the floor with a right hook to the temple.

My heart thuds to a stop in my chest. "Christ!"

I spring for Destiny and tackle her to the ground. I straddle her and pin her shoulders down. She claws at my face and I feel a nail slice through my cheek.

I grab her arms and pin them to the floor next to her head, a trickle of warm blood courses down my face and drops from my chin onto her T-shirt, where I hover above her.

"No, stop!" she screams. "Get off me!"

"Destiny," I say, "calm down."

"No!" she begs. "God, no. Please."

I glance at Lilah as Destiny kicks and bucks against me. She's just getting her bearings, pulling herself to a sitting position against the couch. She looks through a mask of shock at her sister, writhing on the floor, then back at me.

But then Destiny stops screaming. A low moan, like a wounded animal, tears up her throat and she twists on her side under me and curls into a fetal position. I ease up my pressure as she wails, a cry from the depths of her soul.

Lilah crawls over and tentatively reaches for her shoulder. There's already a red welt rising on her left cheek. "Destiny?"

Her sister only curls tighter into a ball.

I lift myself off her and touch Lilah's face. She flinches away in pain as I brush my fingers over the bruise. "You okay?"

She nods, but her attention doesn't leave Destiny. She pulls her sister's shoulders into her lap. "Something's wrong."

Destiny's still moaning and a trail of spit trickles from her open mouth onto the carpet.

"I'll call an ambulance," I say, grabbing my phone and dialing 911.

It's only a few seconds later, after I've given the dispatcher the address and said it's a medical emergency, that I hear sirens cut through the still outside. A cop is the first to arrive, followed a few minutes later by an ambulance. By that time, Destiny's cries have trailed off. She's basically unresponsive when the paramedics check her over and load her onto a stretcher. Lilah goes with them to the hospital, and when the dust settles, it's just me and the cop. His name is Steve Shaw and he was a few years ahead of me at Oak Crest High.

He takes a look around the room, then looks at me. "Okay, Bran. Why don't you start from the beginning and tell me what happened here."

If I were a good person, I'd tell him everything. But I'm not. "Destiny Morgan works for Mom at the bar. We…dated."

He gives me a skeptical look, because everyone in this town knows me and my reputation. "You mean you had sexual relations with her."

It's not a question, but I nod. "Things didn't end well. She thought I was into her sister. I was worried and came by to check on them and Destiny had some kind of breakdown."

"I was the first responder, but someone else had already broken the outside door in."

Again, not a question, but he's clearly waiting for an answer. "That was me. I heard them fighting and Destiny wouldn't let Lilah open the door for me."

"Did either Miss Morgan have reason to be frightened of you?"

The truth is, Destiny was terrified, but only after I was restraining her. It was almost as if it triggered some memory and she went somewhere else in her head.

I shake my head. "No, I don't think so."

"Then why wouldn't she have just let you in? Why did you feel you had to break the door down?"

My lips press hard together. "She just didn't want me near Lilah. She was jealous."

His gaze becomes more focused on my eyes, looking for the lie. "Did she have reason to be?"

Moment of truth. "I kissed Lilah."

If he figures out how old Lilah is and decides to poke into it, I could end up in a world of hurt.

He takes a deep breath but manages to contain the eye roll. "Regular Payton Place."

"We were in L.A. and her friend was on that show, *The Voice*. We got caught up in the moment and I kissed her. It was caught on camera and Destiny saw. She went batshit, threatened to move them away from here," I say, gesturing at the boxes. "I heard them fighting and I was worried for Lilah's safety, so I broke in the door."

"And then Destiny just..." He shakes his head. "What?"

"She was screaming at me, then she swung at Lilah. Nearly knocked her out. I jumped on her and she started screaming, then crying. Went from there into what you saw."

He nods slowly and pulls out a pad, jotting some notes. "Don't go anywhere, Bran. If everything checks out, then you'll be fine, but I need to talk to the sister first."

I start toward the stairs. "Got a tool kit in my car. I'm gonna just nail this door shut for now."

He takes one last look around and follows me to the door. "I'll be in touch."

CHAPTER 26

Lilah

They gave Destiny something in the ER that seemed to calm her down and her moaning stopped. I don't even want to know what horrific thing she was reliving. It took them most of the night, but eventually they found her a bed in the psych ward. I guess by law, they can't turn away a psych case, even if there's no insurance.

I'm still not exactly sure what happened. It's a little bit blurry in my head. She kept screaming that Bran had raped me, then all of a sudden, she's punching me, like something just snapped and she went into self-defense mode.

There have been a series of people that have come in to look over Destiny's file. A few of them asked me questions about whether Destiny has any allergies, whether she uses recreational drugs or alcohol, whether she's had any psychiatric treatment in the past, what our current living situation is, if we have other family, and one woman who introduced herself as Destiny's therapist wanted to know about our childhood and our parents. I told her everything I could think of. They let me stay with

Destiny all day and brought me a tray at lunch and dinner. The cop from the house came and asked some questions a little while ago. Finally, as it starts getting dark outside Destiny's window, the nurse tells me I have to go.

I call Jon and wait at the main entrance for him to come for me.

"Hey," he says when I slide into the passenger seat of the Mustang. So much has happened in the last twenty-four hours, it feels like a year since I've been here.

"Hey," I parrot, my mind too numb to come up with anything else.

"Mom wants you to stay with us for a while," he says. "You good with that?"

I slump into the seat and nod.

He leaves me alone for the short ride to his house and when we get there, Bethany goes into super-mom mode when she sees the bruise on my face.

"Oh you poor dear," she says. "You're safe now. I've got the guest room made up and you'll stay with us until your sister recovers."

I nod, because I don't have the energy to think right now.

Jon comes with me to my room and we sprawl across the double bed. "You didn't miss much in algebra," he says, "but I'll let you copy my homework."

"Thanks."

"We got knocked out of the playoffs last night, so football's officially over."

I roll my head to look at him. "Good thing, or bad thing?"

"Good, I think," he says with a nod. "I'm ready for a break."

"Okay. Great." I turn my face back to the ceiling and hook an elbow over my eyes. My lids are all of a sudden too heavy to hold up.

Until Jon says, "And I kissed Troy."

I spring to a sit and look down at him. "Redwood linebacker Troy?"

He smiles and nods.

"And?" I wave to his privates. "Zing or no zing?"

That goofy grin pulls at his mouth. "Definite zing."

I hold up a hand and he high fives me. "You slut."

He sits up and windshield wipers a finger at me. "Hey, hey, hey…none of that. It was just a kiss."

"For now," I say.

"What about you?" he asks. "What's going on with Cradle Robber?"

Bran.

I've tried to keep my mind where it belongs right now, on my sister, but all day it's crept to him. I left him standing in the apartment with a cop last night. I don't know what happened after that. He texted this morning to say he'd boarded up our door. He wants me to let him know when I need to get in. I texted back "Thanks," and that was it.

"I don't know," I answer honestly.

❖

It's been four days. I've gone to school and work, and visited Destiny when I can. Bethany is insisting I stay with them until Destiny's home, but the truth is, I'll go out of my fucking mind and end up in the hospital bed next to my sister if I have to be there one more day. It's unnatural for any group of people to be this happy.

So, I text Bran from work, tell him I'm ready for him to let me into the apartment.

I expect him to go over and open it up for me. What I don't expect is to walk out of the market and find his car on the curb outside and him leaning against the door. There's a definite December chill in the air, and he's wearing a well worn black leather jacket over a blue hoodie and jeans.

And, God, he's incredible.

It's easy to forget when I'm away from him, but the sight of him steals my breath.

"You ready?" he asks, shoving off his car.

No. There's no way to be ready for the wave of desire that overwhelms me every time I'm near him. "Yeah."

He opens the door for me and I slide in. He climbs in his side and watches the road ahead as we pass Sam Hill on the way to our apartment. When I see our door, I bust out laughing. I expected a few two by four scraps nailed over the opening, but he's replaced the outer door with a steel security door.

"Wanted to be sure no one messed with your stuff. Especially since you were nice enough to pack it all up for them."

"We don't have anything but a busted TV. They could have it."

He looks at me for a second before swinging open his door. He produces a key from his pocket and turns it in the locks, then hands it to me and stands back.

"After you."

I climb the stairs and Bran follows. At the top, I pull out my key and let us in.

Everything is as we left it, boxes littering the floor and surfaces. Except, there's a new TV on the table in the corner. I look at him.

"Mom had an extra." He goes over and turns it on, then picks up a remote and pokes at it. "The episodes of *The Voice* we were at are on the TiVo."

He clicks play and the finals start.

"Zip to Lo," I say as I drop onto the couch.

He pulls off his jacket and slings it over the arm of the couch before sitting at the other end and doing as I ask. We watch her first song and I get shivers listening to her hit notes I could only dream of. And when he zips to the intro for her original song, and they say my name, the rush makes me shudder.

"Did you see?" Bran asks. "You've been number one since the show."

I look at him and he gives me half a smile. I've been so caught up in everything else, I hadn't thought about the fact that they released that single. Something I wrote is being heard by millions of people. I turn my attention back to the screen just as the camera pans to the audience…and catches me and Bran mauling each other right in the middle of the crowded auditorium.

My fingers dig into my knees and I feel heat creep up my face. Lo hits the final note and Bran clicks off the TV.

He stands and grabs his jacket, flinging it over his shoulder. "I'll leave you alone. Lock the doors behind me."

I bound from my seat. "Don't go!"

He turns slowly and heat blazes from his dark gaze as it rakes over me. "I can't be here without needing to kiss you, Lilah."

I take a step toward him. "Then kiss me."

For several beats of my racing heart, he stands at the door doing battle with himself.

"Please," I say.

It's barely a whisper, but it blows the smolder in his eyes into an inferno. In two long strides he's on me, and I'm being crushed in his strong arms and devoured by his mouth. His kiss demands everything I have, and I give it to him. I open wide and give myself up to his desire. There's no way something can burn this bright and not spontaneously combust. I expect to burst into flames at any second.

But when I start tugging at his clothes, desperate to feel him inside me again, he peels my hands away and steps back. "You have no idea how badly I want to fuck you blind right now, but if we're going to do this, I need everyone on board."

"Destiny," I say when what he's saying clicks in my head. I raise my eyebrows, challenging him. "You think she's going to get on board with you fucking me blind?"

He barks a laugh. "I don't need her on board with the specifics, only the basic concept. I need to know she's not going to have my sorry ass thrown in jail."

"There's nothing sorry about your ass, Bran."

He shakes his head at me. "Exactly what I'm afraid the rest of the inmates are going think."

"Besides," I say with a sigh. "I'm not sure Destiny's going to get on board with anything."

His kiss swollen lips press into a line. "We'll just have to convince her. When she's better."

I slip my T-shirt off and toss it at him. "You're sure I can't convince *you*?"

He snatches it out of the air and presses it to his face, closing his eyes and breathing deep. "I'm trying to do the right thing by everyone and you are fucking with my resolve."

God, he's right. I'm a horrible person. Destiny is fighting for her sanity and here I am trying to get laid.

He turns for the door, taking my shirt with him. "You should come back to the bar now that you're famous. Been saving your seat."

"I'll think about it," I say as he retreats down the stairs.

The steel door at the bottom bangs shut and I go to the window and watch him cross the street. He pulls on his jacket on the way to his car, and before he drops into his seat, he lifts my shirt to his face again and breathes deep.

He pulls away and leaves me aching for him.

CHAPTER 27

Bran

Lilah comes into the bar at eight thirty and my heart swells. I've been a good boy for the last week and a half since the kiss at her apartment and kept my hands off. But it's been an epic struggle.

Tonight, she's bundled into a jacket with a furry collar and I think I'm safe...until she peels it and the scarf underneath off. She's in boots past her knees, a short tight skirt and a long-sleeved, gauzy button-down blouse that clings in all the right places. At my perusal, her nipples tighten into nubs and I smile. I still affect her too. Good to know.

My body does what it always does in her presence, and I spend the next four hours trying to tame my raging boner.

Lilah stays until closing tonight, and it suddenly hits me that all those nights I thought she was leaving to see someone, she probably had a curfew. A stab of panic slices through my gut with the reality of Lilah's age. Sixteen. God, that was a long time ago. But I must be getting used to the idea, because the panic isn't incapacitating anymore and it passes quickly.

My sister Brenda is covering nights until Carol comes back, which should be just after New Year's. She punches out a little before one and turns off the lit OPEN sign in the window on her way out. And then it's just Lilah and me.

"How's Destiny?" I ask as she packs away her guitar.

"Better. We have a session together with her therapist on Monday and then they might let her come home." She looks up at me with a spark of panic. "I know you want her stamp of approval, but what if she says no? What if she still wants to move?"

I brace my hands on the bar to keep from leaping over it to comfort her. "Then we'll deal with it."

"How?"

"Maybe we just have to wait until you turn eighteen." My heart turns to stone in my chest at the thought and I pray it doesn't come to that.

Her panic ebbs and her whole face softens. "You would wait over a year for me?"

She looks suddenly so innocent and the breath leaves my lungs. "I would wait forever for you. I've survived snipers and landmines, and I honestly never fully understood why we were even there. But with you, my eyes are wide open. *I'm* making the choice, and whatever the consequences are, I'm ready to handle them. If I have to wait, I'll wait. But I'll never quit you, Lilah. I can't."

She comes slowly around to my side of the bar and loops her arms around my neck, and when she pulls me into a kiss, I'm helpless to stop her. Now that I have her in my arms, I'm totally unwilling to let her go. We kiss for long enough that she finally tips her head back, gasping for air. My lips skim her long throat to her pulse point and I flick my tongue there, causing her to gasp. But when she reaches for the throbbing bulge in my jeans, I know I've taken this too far.

"I've been wanting to fuck you on this bar since the first time you walked in here," I growl. I let her go and back away. "And I will, but not tonight."

She takes a deep breath and straightens her clothes. "All this for Destiny's approval?"

"I used to think what I did didn't matter—that no one gave a shit." I start switching off lights. "But I met a girl a few months back, and she made me not want to be such a fucking dick all the time. So I'm trying." Once the room is dark, I pull her into my arms. "I'm bound to fuck up here and there, because that's what I do, but I'm going to at least try to get this off on the right foot."

I kiss her again, slow and deep, then guide her to the door. I grab her guitar on the way and toss it in my backseat. When we reach her apartment, I kiss her again. "Lock up and text me when you're going to bed."

"Why?"

I grin. "Because that's when I'll be jacking off and imagining myself all up inside you."

She leans in slowly and lays a soft, warm kiss on my mouth. "You don't have to imagine."

I tip my forehead into hers. "Yes I do. For now."

She takes a deep breath then shoulders out her door. She leans in before she closes it. "I like you better when you're bad."

I hand her guitar out to her and she turns for the apartment. I wait for her to disappear behind the security door and the light to turn on upstairs before I pull away.

She texts me a selfie fifteen minutes later. It's from the waist up and she's naked, her perfect round tits pointing at the camera and her nipples pricked into tight nubs. One hand is twisted into the blond hair strewn across her pillow. She's all bedroom eyes and pouty lips and that look tightens my balls.

I grab my key and storm to the door, because I fucking need her more than oxygen right now. I ache all over with want, and I know she won't turn me away when I pound on her door and take what I need from her.

But my newfound conscience stops me in my tracks before I even get the door open. I made a promise to myself and part of being the guy she deserves is keeping it. So I do exactly what I told her I would. I drop onto the couch, pull out my throbbing cock, and go to town. Because it's the only way I'm going to be able to keep that promise.

CHAPTER 28

Lilah

When Destiny's therapist called and asked me to come in for a session, I thought we'd be talking about Destiny. We're not. Destiny's not even in the room.

Mary The Therapist looks at me expectantly, waiting for my answer.

"I don't really see what this has to do with anything," I say, evading.

She leans forward, her elbows on her knees. "It has to do with how trauma from your past manifests in your life today."

"But what does that have to do with Destiny?"

Mary's face goes all concern. "You and your sister were subjected to some horrible experiences by the people who you instinctively trusted to protect you. That leaves scars. In situations where siblings have shared trauma, they can feed off each other triggers."

"So…you're saying what happened to Destiny is *my* fault. I triggered something?"

She springs back, surprised. "No. No," she says with wave of her hand, as if erasing the thought from an imaginary whiteboard. "This isn't about assigning blame. It's about helping both you girls understand what happened so you can develop healthy coping mechanisms."

I take a deep breath. "So, what are you asking me, really? Because 'Tell me about your childhood' is a pretty broad topic."

"From what I understand, it was pretty tumultuous."

I slump into the couch. "Understatement."

"What do you remember about your parents?"

"That they were too busy getting stoned to care about anything else."

"Including you girls?"

I look a dagger at her. "Especially us girls."

"Where are they now?"

"In jail."

"Both of them?" she asks, jotting a note.

"That's what happens when you burn down half a city block cooking meth."

Her eyes lift to me and search my face. "You know everything you say in this room is confidential, Lilah."

I huff out a derisive laugh. "So I'm supposed to what? Confess how much I hated my parents? How I'm glad they're in prison? How I wish they were dead?"

Her eyes twitch and she leans forward. "Do you?"

"Do I what?" I ask, flopping onto the back of the couch, a frustrated itch under my skin making me antsy.

"Wish they were dead?"

I shrug. "Wouldn't that make me just like every other American teenager?"

She sets her pad down and looks at me a long moment. "Let's talk about the night of the fire. Tell me everything you remember."

"I already told you everything the day Destiny came here."

"There are pieces missing, though, Lilah. I think they might be important."

I squirm in my corner of the couch, fighting to stay seated against the sudden compulsion to run. "I came home from school early. Our parents blew up the house and we got trapped upstairs by the fire. We had to run through the fire to get out."

"How old was Destiny then?" she asks.

I roll my eyes to the ceiling, adding in my head. "Nineteen, I guess."

"And did she still live at home?"

"She…" I shake my head as the question jumbles in my mind. "She was gone a lot, but yeah." Her searching gaze feels like it's burning the skin off my face, so I cover it with my hand.

"Why did you come home from school early?" she asks after forever.

"My best friend and I got suspended for gambling."

"And who do you remember seeing when you got home? Was Destiny there?"

My heart's beating out of control. I can't sit anymore so I stand and pace a circle around the room. "She wasn't home when I got there."

"Who was? Did you see anyone in the house?"

"Dad and…some guy." I shake my head. "But there were always people I didn't know."

"Did you see them afterward, outside the house? Your dad and the man?"

I hug myself tight and stop pacing at the window, looking out at the drizzle dampening the sidewalks outside. The ants under my skin are making me twitch, but no matter how much I rub, they won't go away.

I search my memory, and in it, see fire trucks rolling up the house, sirens blaring. On the sidewalk, in the glow of the flames shooting into the night sky, I see Mom and some neighbors. I don't see Dad.

I shake my head at the image.

Night sky…

But the fire happened during the day. I came home around lunchtime and went straight upstairs. It was only a few minutes later that Destiny and I were running through the flames to the front door.

I'm sure of it.

"Where were you when the fire broke out?"

"I…" …don't remember.

"Do you remember how you got out?" she presses.

I rub harder at the ants under my skin. "I told you. Destiny got some wet blankets and we ran through the fire."

"So, she *was* there."

I spin on her. "Why are you asking me all this? Destiny's your patient, not me!"

"Why don't you sit, Lilah. Can I get you some water? Or something else to drink?"

"Where's Destiny?" I say, crossing to the door and opening it. The small waiting room is empty.

"She's in her room. And, to answer your question, I'm asking you because she's having difficulty recalling all the details about the night of the fire. It seems to be the focal point of whatever trauma caused her to break down last week. I'm just trying to sort through some things so I can help her."

I close the door and lean against it. "We were trapped. We thought we were going to die. It was terrifying."

She nods slowly. "That's totally understandable. When one's survival is threatened, the whole system goes into survival mode and decisions aren't always conscious. Details blur and actions don't get recorded in short term memory. In extreme cases, when the trauma threatens the psyche, the mind will deliberately block the memory as a defense."

"You think Destiny's doing that?"

"Neither one of you seems to have a clear recollection of events that night."

I move back to the couch and sit. "How can I help her?"

"Anything you remember could be significant."

I try to trace my steps from the time I got home until the fire, but I only get flashes. A yell. A scream. Water.

A sick feeling settles in my stomach and the ants are itching my skin again.

I was wet, and it was more than the blankets we soaked in the tub. Why was I wet?

The image I sometimes see in my nightmares of blood swirling down drain surfaces in my mind.

There was blood.

I shake my head, shaking off the ants along with the clammy feeling. "I don't remember."

"I'm discharging Destiny," Mary says slowly, "but she'll need to continue to some with outpatient therapy. I'd like to see you separately for a few weeks and then we can work into sessions with the two of you together."

I stand, feeling the need to run again. "Why do I need to come?"

She smooths her skirt as she slowly gains her feet, then moves to her desk. "You've clearly both suffered a horrible trauma. Destiny's never going to truly recover until she can face what it was."

"I'm fine," I say, shaking my head again. It just keeps doing that.

She pulls open a laptop on her desk and looks over the screen. "Will Mondays after school work for you?" she asks as if I said nothing.

"I have to work."

She looks up at me. "What is your schedule? Do you have a day off?"

"Not if I can help it. We're broke. And, also, we have no insurance, so I don't think we can afford to see you."

"Let's not concern ourselves with that," she says, shaking her hand in the air without looking up from her screen. "I could see you Saturday mornings if that's the only day you're available."

"I still don't understand how me coming here is going to help Destiny."

"So, nine o'clock?" she says, looking at me with raised eyebrows.

And I get that she's not taking no for an answer.

When I get to Destiny's room, she's ready to go. We take the bus down the hill to town and when she sees the security door, she looks a question at me.

"Bran," I say as I turn the key in the lock, a little afraid to bring him up.

Her lips purse, but then she nods.

"I've got a box of mac and cheese that I can make for dinner, if you want," I say on the way up the stairs.

"Okay."

It's the first word out of her mouth since she said hi when I walked into her hospital room, and I'm not sure if

I should try to make her talk or not. There was no instruction manual for my slightly crazy sister in the discharge paperwork, so I'm flying by the seat of my pants.

"There might be an apple I can slice to go with it," I say.

Once we're through the door, she looks at the boxes, but doesn't say anything.

"I only unpacked the things I needed," I volunteer.

I wasn't sure if we were staying or going, and I didn't want her to come home and be upset that I'd unpacked everything.

She goes to the kitchen and starts filling our only pot with water.

"I'll get that, Destiny," I say, following her. "You should just rest."

"That's all I've been doing." She sets the pot on the stove and cranks on the burner. "I'm supposed to be taking care of you."

"I'm fine. It's my turn to look after you for a change."

She braces her hands on the counter without turning. "What did Mary say to you?"

My heart jumps in my chest. "She just…" I shake my head. "Nothing really."

Finally, she turns and leans against the counter, watching my face as she says, "She wanted to know about the fire."

It's not a question, but I nod anyway.

"What did you tell her?"

I shake my head and drop into a kitchen chair. "When I tried to remember what happened…" I shrug. "Maybe I just hate Mom and Dad so much that I blocked it all out, but I can't really remember much."

I expect her typical concerned squint, but what I see in her eyes instead is relief. "You don't have to go to that appointment, Lilah. She can't force you to."

"Good. She kind of creeps me out." But even as I say it, I know that's not entirely accurate. *She* didn't creep me out as much as the loose fringes of memory I couldn't weave into a whole tapestry.

"Good," she repeats with a nod, turning back to the pasta. "Then it's settled."

While the pasta cooks, she starts unpacking the kitchen things back into the cupboards.

"So, I guess this means we're not leaving?" I say.

She shoots me a glance. "I think I'll see if Ambling Rose is looking for any help."

I smile at the idea. "You should bake something and take it over when you go. Even if they're not looking for anyone, one taste and they'll hire you on the spot."

She smiles back. "Grandma would roll over in her grave if she thought I was divulging her secret recipes."

I pick up the slightly mealy apple and rinse it in the sink. I grab the carving knife Destiny just unpacked and slice it in half, then quarters. But as I'm cutting the core out, the knife slips and the point digs into my hand. I pull it out and watch a bead of blood pool in my palm. As it grows, the ants start crawling under my skin again.

The image of the sharp point of a knife against Destiny's forehead flashes into my head and I my eyes fix on the white scar there.

Blood on the carpet.

Blood swirling down the drain.

My vision goes red and all I see is blood...

Destiny's on the floor, a spray of blood across her shirt that's not hers. And I'm covered, my hands and my clothes soaked.

I grab some fresh clothes from Destiny's closet and help her to her feet. We make it to the bathroom and I strip, then help Destiny out of what's left of her clothes. She's unsteady and I get in the shower with her to prop her up while I rinse the blood off us both. By the time we finish and I turn off the water, she's starting to get her wits. I sit her on the toilet and she's able to dry herself off.

"Do you smell that?" she says.

And I do—the smell of something burning. I push open the door and the smoke nearly chokes me.

"Oh my god!" I croak, covering my face with my towel.

We yank on our clothes and stumble to the stairs. Flames lick the broken banister and the drapes on the window near the front door are a torch.

"What do we do?" I shout, then start coughing and can't stop.

Destiny pushes me down and tells me to stay there before staggering to her room. She comes out with the blankets off the bed. She takes them to the bathroom and I hear her coughing too as she turns on the tub. She comes back a minute later and throws a wet blanket on top of me. "Wrap it around you, including your head."

I get to my feet and struggle to drape the heavy blanket over my head, finally tugging it tightly around the front of me and leaving just a hole to peek through.

"Ready? she says between coughs.

I nod and she starts down the stairs.

"We're going to have to run through it," she says as the heat intensifies. "You go first."

"I can't!" I scream. The fire is louder now, and so hot I feel my skin tighten even through the wet blanket.

"You have to! I'll be right behind you!"

I shake my head, terror petrifying me into stone and gluing my feet to the stair.

"We can't wait!" she yells, then grabs my blanket and starts dragging me.

When I realize we're going no matter what, I grab onto her and start running. Flames lick at the edges of my blanket and the heat is so intense I'm sure I'm burning alive, but I run and don't stop until we're outside.

The sirens are so loud they scramble my brain, and as we move down the walk, I see Mom, sitting cross-legged on the sidewalk, staring at the burning house. Her expression is totally blank, but as we pass, she says, "It went faster than I thought it would," without taking her eyes off the building inferno.

I know that's supposed to be some kind of apology, but Destiny and I drop the blankets and just keep walking.

I slow at the corner and start to turn to watch as the emergency crews screech to a stop in front of our house, but Destiny grabs my hand and yanks me across the street. "We've got to get out of here."

"Lilah?" She's got my shoulders in her hands. She starts shaking me. "Lilah!

I drop the bloody apple and realize tears are coursing down my cheeks. I brace my hands on the counter until my legs will carry me to the table, where I collapse into a chair. "I remembered."

She grimaces. "What do you think you remember?"

I'm all questions and no answers. I grab onto the first one that spins past in the cyclone of my mind. "Why did we run? Why didn't we stay with Mom when we got out of the house?"

"She was going to jail. CPS would have split us up if they knew we existed, stuck you in some foster home or whatever."

I know there's more she's not telling me by the fear that flashes in her eyes. "I remember a knife…the one from under my bed. I see it against your forehead in my dreams sometimes," I say, pressing my finger to the place on my forehead where the scar is on hers. My heart is struggling to keep a rhythm and I hold my breath. "Did I do that to you? I can't remember."

Her eyes widen. "God, no, Lilah!" She shakes her head as if shaking away a memory. "No, it wasn't you."

"Then who?" I know it's probably wrong for me to push her when she's just gotten home, but I have to know. "I keep seeing blood... a lot of blood."

She stands and shakes her head again. "I'm not doing this, Lilah. Just let it lie."

She disappears up the hall and closes the door to her room as the macaroni on the stove boils over.

CHAPTER 29

Bran

I'm not sure how to play this since Destiny's been home, so I've let Lilah take the lead. I'm trying not to read too much into it, but I've felt on the edge of a panic attack since she came in last night to play at the bar. She was distant, not like she was angry, or even upset, but more distracted. Or really, haunted.

I gave her space, because it's all I really can do. She and Destiny have some things to work out. My biggest fear is that I'm the root of it, and as hard as I've fallen for Lilah, I can't be responsible for driving a wedge between her and Destiny. Which is why I told her I needed Destiny on board with this. I'm just not quite sure how to make that happen.

My phone wakes me early Saturday and I pick it up and squint at the screen. When I see Lilah's number, I snap it up.

"Hey."

There's a long pause. "Do you have time to talk?" she finally asks.

"Yeah. Absolutely." I climb out of bed and rake yesterday's jeans up from the floor next to my bed. "Should I come by or…?"

"Yeah. I'll meet you out front."

"On my way," I say, tugging them up my legs. I disconnect and find a fresh T-shirt, then yank on my leather jacket on the way out the door.

When I pull up, she's already waiting outside. I reach across to open my passenger door and she climbs in.

"Where to?" I ask.

She shrugs and slumps into the seat.

I roll away from the curb and drive. "Everything okay with Destiny?"

Finally, she looks at me. She looked tired yesterday and it made me wonder about her nightmares. Today, she's worse; purple crescents under red-rimmed, lifeless eyes. I know that look. She hasn't slept in a while.

"I'm not sure."

"She hasn't…you know, had any meltdowns or anything, has she?"

She shakes her head. "We've never talked about the night our house burnt down. I always thought it was because…" She shrugs then lifts her gaze to mine. "You know that scar on her forehead?"

I nod.

She lowers her gaze and watches her fingers fidget with the strings of her hoodie. "She got the cut that night. I used to keep a big carving knife under my bed because there were some scary people squatting at our house most of the time. I've seen the tip of that knife making the cut in my dreams. I was afraid to bring up the fire because I was afraid I'd hurt Destiny even though I couldn't remember."

I don't like the thought of Lilah feeling like she needed a knife to protect herself in her own home, and again find myself wishing her parents bodily harm.

"I asked her on Monday when we got home. She said it wasn't me. But…" She shakes her head. "Something happened with Destiny and me the night of the fire that I can't remember. The thing is, every time I try, I feel sick and ants start crawling under my skin."

"Have you asked her?"

"She won't talk about it." She rubs her eyes then looks at me. "I'm scared, Bran. I'm not really sure if I want to know."

I snag her eyes with my gaze and hold them. "Only you know if you're ready to face down your demons, Lilah."

She tips her head against the window as if it's too heavy to hold up.

We're passing the shelter at the downhill end of the park and I pull over. "You want to walk?" I ask, nodding at the path that winds up the hill to the playground up top.

She looks at me a long second, then pushes out her door. I climb out and take her hand. She wraps her fingers tightly around mine, but her skin doesn't scorch through mine the way it usually does. She feels clammy, and there's a tremor in her hand.

The last stubborn leaves of fall are now curled in dry brown heaps at the side of the path, crunching under our feet as we start up the hill.

"I talked to Destiny's therapist on Monday," Lilah says, watching the dead husks swirl around our feet in the crisp breeze. "She was asking about the night of the fire. She thinks Destiny needs to remember what happened, but I think she already does."

I try to follow what she's saying. "You think Destiny's pretending not to remember?"

She pulls her hand from mine and shoves them into her hoodie pockets. "I only remember parts of what happened that night. She seems nervous that I might start to remember more."

"Maybe if Destiny's trying not to remember, you should be glad you don't," I say wishing that I could forget half of the things that I relive in my nightmares. "Some things are better left alone."

She watches the path unfold in front of us and leads me to a bench under a group of leafless trees. For a minute, she just looks at it, but then she brushes the leaves off and sits. I sit next to her and loop my arm over her shoulders. My heart releases the breath it's been holding when she leans into me and lays her head on my shoulder.

"I'm supposed to see her therapist again later this morning. Destiny doesn't want me to go."

I tip my face into her hair and breathe deeply. "I think what you choose to do is up to you, not Destiny."

She presses tighter to my side. "I want to. Maybe she can help me remember."

"But you said you weren't sure you wanted to."

She lifts her head and fixes me in her gaze. "But I think I have to."

I brush my fingertips over her cold cheek and along the line of her jaw. When I pull her into a kiss, she kisses me back.

"Will you take me?" she asks, leaning into my side again.

"Of course." I would do anything for her. All she has to do is ask. But if this therapist ends up destroying her by digging up whatever this memory is her mind is protecting her from, I'll never forgive myself.

CHAPTER 30

Lilah

Bran walks me to the door of the hospital. "Do you want me to come in with you?"

I shake my head. "Will you wait?"

His eyes grow darker and search mine. "Of course, Lilah. I'm not going anywhere."

I take both of his hands in mine, and despite the fact that my heart is about to explode, it warms with the love and concern I see in his gaze. "Knowing that is the only thing that gives me the strength to do this."

He kisses me and when our lips part, I back away and turn for the door. When I get to Mary's waiting room, it's empty. Her office door is open.

"I'm so glad you decided to come, Lilah," she says, appearing in the doorway.

I mentally brace myself. Now that I'm here, I have to follow through. "I remembered some things after I was here."

She nods encouragingly and leads me into her office, closing the door behind us. She takes a seat in the wingchair as I lower myself onto the couch. "This session is yours, Lilah. We can talk about what you remembered, or anything else that you want to talk about."

I squirm to get comfortable in the corner of the cushions and lean my elbows on my knees, watching my toes turn first in, then out. "I've had flashes blood for a while—a knife pressed against Destiny's forehead, but I don't remember whose hand it was in." I look up at her. "I asked her Monday and she says it wasn't mine."

"Why would you think it was?"

"It was a carving knife I kept under my bed when creepy people started squatting in our house."

"Because you were scared?"

I nod.

"So you see this knife cutting Destiny, but not who's holding it?"

I rub my forehead. "There are a whole lot of things that don't make sense. I see a lot of blood—too much to be just from Destiny's cut. We were covered with it. We cleaned up in the bathroom and when we came out, the house was burning and we had to run through the fire to get out." Things are scrambling in my mind as I try to piece it together. "I think our mom might have set the fire."

"While you were in the house?" she asks, keeping both her tone and expression carefully neutral.

I nod. "But I don't think she meant to hurt Destiny and me. I just don't know why she would have done that."

"The blood," she says. "If it wasn't Destiny's, who do you think it belonged to?"

I shake my head. "I can't remember. I don't even know how I ended up covered in it."

She leans toward me, her hand on her knee. "Do you want to remember, Lilah?"

I take a deep breath and rub at the itch in my arms. "Yes and no."

"If you're serious about remembering, it's possible hypnosis could get you past the block in your memory."

Cold terror grasps my heart and squeezes, sending a shiver wracking my body. "How would that work?"

"It's really just helping you to find a meditative state where things are clearer."

"But I would be awake…remember what I remember?"

She nods. "You will always be in full control."

I'm shaking as I stand and move to the window. Her office looks out the front of the building, and Bran is out there. A light drizzle has started and he's pacing the parking lot near his car, seemingly oblivious to the fact that he's getting wet. He stops and looks toward the door I entered through, then paces some more.

I turn back to Mary. "Okay. What do I do?"

"Just have a seat," she says, motioning to the couch.

I move toward it. "Should I lay down?"

"Only if you want to," she says.

Instead, I curl into the corner and pull my knees to my chest.

She takes me through the basic drill and says at any point if I want to bring myself back to a full conscious state, I only have to count backwards from five.

"Ready?" she asks me.

I nod.

She briefly goes over the instructions again and then counts to five.

"Are you comfortable, Lilah?" she asks.

"I don't feel any different," I say, honestly.

"Then we're right on track," she says. "I'm going to ask you a few questions. Feel free to answer only what you're comfortable with."

"Okay."

"We already talked about your expulsion from school," she starts. "You got home, then what happened?"

My mind slips effortlessly back to that gray day. I feel the mist collecting on my face as I trudge toward home.

I'm walking alone because someone from Lo's group home came for her, but the school couldn't reach my parents to talk to them about my suspension, so they finally let me go on my own. When I get to the house, I can hear yelling from the sidewalk, which is nothing new.

Someone's always yelling. Usually Dad. Stoned people aren't as mellow as you'd think.

I walk in and find the source of the yelling is some massive guy I've never seen before. He's younger than Dad and has a raised red scar down his left cheek.

"You said that last week!" he screams, spittle flying from his mouth into Dad's face.

Dad's in the same stained wife-beater he's been wearing for the last week, the fringe of his stringy dark hair long and wild around his face. And he's stoned, as usual. I can tell by the way he just stares at the guy for too long before answering. "I fucked up, but I'll get your cash."

When I close the door behind me, they both look up.

"What are you looking at?" Dad snarls.

I take the stairs two at a time up to my room. When I glance down from the top, the guy is watching me.

"I know who has money," Dad says, but I don't wait to hear who. I close my bedroom door and lock it, then curl onto my mattress on the floor and press my pillow over my head.

The bang a few minutes later sounds like something exploding, even through my pillow, I toss it aside and hear Destiny scream, "Get the fuck out of here!"

"Your pop says you're stashing cash. He owes me." It's muffled through the wall, but there's no mistaking the gravel voice of the guy from downstairs.

"I don't have any cash," Destiny says, but it's a lie. She's been working secretly at night and putting the money away to get us out of here.

There's another crash, things being tossed.

"You don't want to give me the cash?" the guy bellows. "I got another idea how your pop can settle his debt."

When Destiny screams, I grab my knife and move to the hall. Dad's not there. The wood of Destiny's door frame is splintered around the latch.

The huge guy has Destiny pinned against the wall with a massive hand across her throat. He's torn her leggings and underwear and is his pushing down his pants. Her face is purple and she's choking out garbled sounds as she tries to push him away.

There's a second I can't make a sound, but when the guy groans, I finally find my voice.

"Get off her!"

He looks over his shoulder at me. "I'll get off her when I'm done. Then your dad's gonna finish paying me back when I fuck you too."

His dick out of his pants. It's hard and purple. I've never seen one like that before and there's a second all I can do is stare.

"You like what you see, little girl? How 'bout you come here and suck it." He grabs Destiny's hair and knocks her head hard against the wall twice. She goes down in a heap and he lunges for my arm. I swing out with the knife. Because my attention is so focused between his legs, that's where the point lands. It sinks through the hairy white flesh where his leg meets his body.

"You little bitch!" he bellows, swinging a fist into my face. It connects and I feel a firecracker go off in my cheek. I stagger back, but I have a death grip on the knife and it rips through his leg when I pull it out.

My ass hits the floor as blood spurts in a stream from the gash in his leg, just like in the movies. He comes for me again, but stumbles when his leg won't hold him. He goes down on a knee, then drops to his hands.

"You fucking cunt!" he growls, but it doesn't have the threat behind it now. It's more a mix of horrified disbelief. He makes another grab for me and gets my leg, but when I kick out and slash at his arm with the knife, he howls and rolls onto his back, pressing a hand to where blood is still gushing from his leg.

"What the fuck!"

Dad's voice comes from behind me and I spin, the bloody knife still in my hand. His eyes are wild, and standing in the splintered door, he looks just like Jack Nicholson in that scene from *The Shining*.

I drop the knife and backpedal to the wall, barely caring that I'm only a few inches from the bleeding guy. He's pale now, and his screams have tapered into groans.

"Leave her alone." Destiny's voice is a choked rasp.

When I look toward her, she's pulling herself to her feet, her leggings torn and hanging from one thigh. Dad starts toward me, but Destiny lunges for the knife. She's too unsteady, though, and goes down on the floor.

Dad scoops the knife off the bloody carpet with one hand and fists his other into her hair. He presses the tip to her forehead. "This what you wanted? What was your plan? Gonna slit your old man's throat?"

I curl into a ball and press my eyelids shut tight when a trickle of blood starts down Destiny's forehead. My heart's pounding in my throat, choking off my scream.

I didn't save her. Dad is going to kill us both.

But then there's an earsplitting crack.

I open my eyes and Mom's standing behind Dad. She's wobbly on her feet, and barely more than a skeleton, with sunken, red rimmed eyes and cracked lips. But in her hand is a crow bar, and on the floor is my dad, blood pouring from a dent in his head just over his right ear.

She drops to the floor on her knees. "Get cleaned up," she says. "Get dressed and go. I got this."

The scene fades and I blink, not sure how much I said out loud.

"Lilah?" Mary asks. "What did you recall?"

"Nothing." I say, an uncontrollable tremor shaking my body.

"I can't help if you don't talk to me."

I feel like I've been hit by a freight train. I hurt all over, and I'm shaking so hard I can barely speak. "My friend is in the parking lot. I need him."

She looks at me a long time before gaining her feet. "I'll walk you out."

CHAPTER 31

Bran

When I see Lilah walking toward me through the drizzle with an older woman, I stride in their direction.

"Are you okay?" I ask when I reach her. She's pale, and looks shell shocked.

She nods but doesn't say anything.

I loop an arm around her shoulder and start guiding her to my car.

"I'll look for you next Saturday, Lilah," the woman says to her back. "Please don't miss."

She doesn't respond.

I help her into my car, then get us the hell out of here. Once we're away from the hospital, I pull to the side of the road. "Talk to me Lilah."

She shakes her head. "I need to talk to Destiny."

Something happened in there and my natural instinct is to protect her, but I can't protect her from her own demons.

When we get to her apartment, I walk her up. I know the situation with Destiny might still be delicate, but Lilah's pretty out of it and I'm not going to chance her breaking her neck on those steep stairs. I know that was the right call when she leans on me for support when we reach the top. She opens the door and I follow her through, my arm firmly around her waist. Destiny is on the couch, Mom's old TV playing a *The Big Bang Theory* rerun. When she sees me there's a flash of anger in her eyes...until she gets a look at her sister. She's off the couch like a shot, crossing the room to us.

"What happened to her?" she demands.

"That's Lilah's place to tell you," I say.

I start to turn Lilah over to her sister, but she wraps her arms around me and presses her face into my neck. "Thank you," she whispers. She holds me for several beats of my pounding heart before her grip loosens, but it's a moment longer before I can force my arms to let her go.

I kiss the top of her head, then draw back. "You two have some things to deal with, and I don't want to make that harder on you than it has to be, but just know, I'll always be here if there's anything you need." I lift my eyes to Destiny's. "Both of you."

I turn for the door and head down the stairs to my car. It's Saturday and I need to get to the bar. But I can't help looking up at Lilah's window before I get in, hoping she and Destiny will be able to help each other through whatever this is.

CHAPTER 32

Lilah

I watch the door well after Bran is gone. Destiny sits next to me on the couch and combs her fingers through my hair and I still watch the spot where he was.

"Bran took me to my appointment with Mary," I finally say.

Her hand stops.

I clear my throat. "I know Dad isn't in jail."

She sighs and shakes her head cautiously. "How much did you remember?" she asks.

I face her. "All of it."

Her face crumples.

"Why didn't you tell me?" I ask, my voice lowering.

"You were so young, and you'd blocked it all out. I didn't want you to remember. I wanted you to be able to grow up without being haunted by that memory."

"Is that why we ran? Why you told me not to look back?"

"Think about it, Lilah. People died. I didn't know what was going to happen with the house...if it was going to burn the bodies or if they would know what happened."

"Do they know?"

"That Dad and that guy were dead before the fire?" She shakes her head. "I watched the news and never saw anything. I guess they figured a couple of tweakers dying in a meth fire wasn't unusual. They probably didn't even investigate."

"What about Mom?"

Her lip curls. "What about her?"

"Is she really in jail?"

She nods. "She belongs there, Lilah. She stopped being our mother then day she started using."

"But they don't know she killed Dad?"

"No."

There's a lump of emotion in my throat that I don't want to feel. "She did that for us, Destiny."

Her jaw tightens. "She did it for herself. You know he hit her, Lilah. You spent years watching it happen."

"But, right then...she saved us."

She stands and moves to the kitchen. "Believe what you want. I know she hasn't given a shit about us for most of our lives."

I know she's right, but all of a sudden, I want to hear it from her. "I want to see her."

Her eyes narrow and she starts shaking her head. "No way, Lilah."

"It's been two years. She's got to be clean now."

"I don't care. She's not our mother anymore."

I know from the look on her face that I'm not going to win this. I take a deep breath and click on the TV.

When I walk into Sam Hill, Bran is behind the bar and every inch of me aches when I see him. I've taken the last five days to pull my shit together. He's texted me every day to check in, but he's given me space.

I set my guitar case on the stool that seems to be mine now and unlatch it.

Bran slides a Coke across the bar to me and sets out a tip jar. "Was hoping I'd see you tonight."

Now that he's snagged my gaze, I can't shake free. He comes slowly around the bar and takes my hand, then pulls me through the kitchen door. He pulls me into his arms and buries his face into my hair. "God, I've missed you."

I sink against him and soak up the feeling of his strong arms holding me close, the warmth of his breath in my hair, the tenderness of his lips on my forehead, down my temple, across my cheekbone, eventually finding my mouth. He kisses me, so slowly, but with every ounce of himself.

Right here, right now, I know this is where I belong.

"I love you," I whisper when he draws away.

"I want so badly to help you, Lilah, but I feel so fucking helpless."

I look up at him and he kisses the tip of my nose. "There's something you can do."

"Anything."

"I need a ride to San Francisco."

I asked Destiny to come with us, but she wouldn't even consider it. She tried to forbid me to come, but I told her I needed this for my sanity.

When I walk into the prison, I'm shaking. Bran has my hand and I'm gripping so hard I'm sure I'm about to snap his fingers. They make me store my bag in a locker and go through a metal detector before they let me into the visitation room.

"I'll be right here if you need me," Bran says, gesturing at a row of chairs near the storage lockers.

I press against him and he wraps me in his arms.

He kisses the top of my head. "I've got you."

"Don't let me go."

"Never," he says, squeezing tighter.

I want to ask him to come with me, but there are things I need to ask my mom that I'm not totally sure I want anyone else, even Bran, hearing. Though, I can't imagine I won't tell him everything at some point.

He kisses me again and I draw away and turn for the door. I walk into a large room with rows of tables and benches bolted to the floor. There are a few tables near the back that are occupied, but the majority are not. I take a seat at the one across from the door and wait. It's a few minutes later that a door in the back opens and a woman walks through. She's skinny enough that her gray jumpsuit hangs off her. Her blond hair is pulled into a ponytail at the base of her neck. When she lifts her head I see Destiny's blue eyes looking at me, hollow, but not quite as dead as the last time I saw them.

I stand as she approaches the table. "Mom."

"God, Lilah. You're so beautiful." She looks like she's deciding if she should shake my hand or hug me or just sit.

This isn't some big, touching reunion. I have no idea what I'm feeling for this woman who was never really my mother. I'm not really even sure if I'm ready for the conversation I have to have to get the answers I need. I sit and she slides into a seat across from me.

"You look okay," I say, only realizing I wish she didn't when I hear the disappointment in the words. I want to know she's suffered at least as much as Destiny and me, but she looks like nothing's ever happened.

"Despite everything," she says, flicking her jumpsuit, "I'm good. How are you and Destiny?"

I glare at her. "There's no point in pretending you care now when you never did before."

Her eyes moisten, but I refuse to let myself feel even a pang of regret for telling her the truth, even if she doesn't want to hear it.

"I need to know what happened the night of the fire."

She looks suddenly uncomfortable and shoots a glance at the guard near the door she came through. "What do you want to know?"

"What did they arrest you for?"

She picks at frayed fingernails. "Your dad wasn't very discreet. The cops had been watching the house for months. When the fire broke out they figured it was a lab explosion."

At the mention of Dad, I see him crumpled on the floor with a bloody dent in his head. "It took me a while to really remember what happened that night."

Her eyes flick to me and then back to her fingernails. "That might be a good thing."

"Destiny had a mental…something…a breakdown or whatever."

Something like concern flashes in her eyes. "Because of that night?"

"You really just asked me that?" I feel rage swirl my insides into a cyclone. "Because of every fucking thing you and Dad did to us."

She lowers her gaze.

There are two answers I need. The sooner I ask the questions, the sooner I can be out of here. "Why didn't you wait to set the fire until Destiny and I were out?"

Her frail body heaves with a deep breath and she hangs her head deeper. "I wasn't thinking clearly."

"Because you were stoned," I spit.

She offers a feeble nod. "I…" She trails off and shakes her head. "I think I forgot you were upstairs. I just knew I needed to burn the bodies before anyone else came in and found them."

"You forgot us." The words are acid leaving my mouth.

She cringes up at me, but doesn't respond.

I push the cyclone of emotions that I don't fully understand away and ask the next question. "Why did you kill Dad?"

There's no doubt she understands what I'm asking when her eyes flick to the guard near the door. She lowers her gaze guiltily. "It just happened."

I shake my head. "None of it 'just happened.' Things like that don't 'just happen.'"

Her eyes narrow. "You think I meant for that to happen?"

"I don't know what I think. All I know is that one second Dad is carving a hole in Destiny's forehead, and the next, there's a hole in his."

She takes a deep breath and the creases ease from her face. "He changed when he started using." She shakes her head. "I guess I did too. I know I didn't do right by you girls. I let him hurt you. When I realized how much, I couldn't live with myself."

"He more than *hurt* us," I say, the fury eating a hole through me at the image of the guy pinning Destiny to the wall.

Her eyes drop to the bleeding cuticle she's been picking at. "I should have stopped it before it went that far."

"You think?" I spit.

She cringes up at me. "Things were complicated."

"They weren't *complicated*," I say, standing. "They were easy. You were our *mother*. Your one job was to take care of us. But the only thing you took care of was your habit. You *forgot* us! Nearly burnt us alive!"

I can't stay here anymore. Just being in the same room as her is making me sick. I spin for the door.

"Lilah, wait!"

I want to keep walking. I want to not care. But I can't stop myself from turning to look at her. She's standing, her hands braced on the table as if she needs the support. "You lit the fire," I say, not even caring who hears. "You trapped Destiny and me in that house to burn. All you've ever given a shit about is yourself."

A tear leaks over her lashes and she drops into her seat like a ton of bricks.

I don't know what she thinks is supposed to happen. If she thinks I'm going to go over there, patting her on the back and telling her not to cry, that everything's okay, she's sorely mistaken.

"Hope you enjoy burning in hell," I say, spinning for the door. "It's the least you deserve."

When I burst through the door, Bran is pacing on the other side. He stops and looks a question at me. I step into his arms and hate the tears that spring to my eyes. I don't want to care enough to spare even a single tear for her. She doesn't deserve it.

He retrieves my things from the locker and guides me to the exit without a word. And even when we're finally alone in the car, he doesn't push me to talk.

I lean back and close my eyes. "I killed a man."

The tears roll down my face as I say it. He pulls me against his shoulder. I cry and he holds me as he drives. I feel his strength. I feel his love. I feel him in my soul, and it spills over into him.

I press my face into his shoulder and start talking, and when I'm done, we're home and rain has started to shower down on us like the tears I finally let myself cry.

And Bran knows everything.

CHAPTER 33

Bran

I knew it was bad. I just never expected it to be *this* bad. I bring Lilah back to my place, because after everything I just heard, I don't think she's ready to handle Destiny in the shape she's in. I lay her on my bed and she curls onto her side. I slide on next to her, lean against the headboard and stroke her hair. There are a few more tears before she falls into a restless sleep. Once her breathing becomes heavy, I get up and call Mom.

"Hey," I say when she answers. "Lilah's going through some shit and I need to be here for her. You okay covering the bar tonight?"

"I got it," she says. "Everything okay?"

"Not really, but it's not mine to talk about."

"She's a good kid," she says.

I want to tell her Lilah hasn't been a kid for a while, but I keep my mouth shut. "I'm just going to let her hang here until she's good to go home."

"Okay, Bran." There's a pregnant pause and I know my mom well enough to know there's more coming. "Just be careful."

I haul a deep breath. "Got it, Ma."

I go back to Lilah and sit, my legs extended and my ankles crossed, my back against the headboard. I watch her sleep and only realize hours have gone by when the sun starts to set outside my window. Finally, just as the room goes dark, she stirs and opens her eyes.

"Hey."

She pulls herself up and rubs the sleep out of her eyes. "How long have I been asleep?"

I glance at my phone screen. "About three hours. Hungry?"

"Yeah," she says, pressing a hand to her stomach.

"I'll pull something together." I stand and hold out my hand. "C'mon."

She lets me haul her off the bed and follows me to the kitchen. I open the fridge and don't find much. "Eggs?"

She smiles a little and the sight lightens my heavy heart. "That actually sounds really good."

I pull a pan down from the rack and crack a few into it. "Plates are behind you," I say, nudging my chin at the cupboard behind her.

She pulls two down and stands with her butt against the counter, looking around the apartment. It strikes me at that moment that she's never been here before.

When they're done, I slide two eggs onto each plate and hand her one. I grab a couple of Cokes from the fridge on my way to the table.

"Mom's covering the bar. I'll stay here with you tonight," I say as we slide into seats at my small kitchen table.

There's a second her gaze catches on mine and sparks, but the spark flares out almost immediately and she just looks worn down. She pokes at her eggs, then carves off a bite. That first bite seems to fuel her appetite and she devours the rest.

"That was good," she says, wiping the back of her hand across her mouth and setting her fork on her plate. "Thanks."

She polishes off her Coke as I lift our plates and drop them on top of a few others in the sink. I grab two more Cokes as she heads to the couch. She picks up the remote and surfs the channels. By the time I make it to the couch and pull her tight to my side, she's stopped on *It's a Wonderful Life*.

Christ, I'd forgotten that Christmas is next week.

I sit and drape my arm across her shoulders and she settles into my side. For the next two hours, as George Bailey goes through hell and back trying to save everything he loves, I hold the thing I love close. I know she has to find her way through this, but I'll do whatever I can to help, even if it's only this.

As the credits start to roll, she yawns. "I slept all afternoon. I shouldn't be tired."

"You've faced down some pretty major demons today. That'll knock the crap out of you."

She presses against me and when her mouth meets mine, I can't stop the shudder. I know she feels it when she draws back and looks into my eyes as if looking for something she lost in there.

I stand and pull her off of the couch by the hand. When we get to my room, I dig a T-shirt out of my drawer. "In case you want to change before bed."

Her eyes widen slightly. "I'm staying here?"

"I'm not going to tell you what to do, Lilah, but if you need some space to deal with what you've remembered, you can have that here. I'll stay tonight, because I need to know you're okay, but beyond that is up to you. I can stay with you or just give you the place and let you decompress here."

She takes the shirt from my hand. "Has anyone ever told you how incredible you are?"

I back toward the door. "I'll be on the couch tonight if you need anything."

She lunges for my hand and tugs me back to her. "I do need something. I need you with me. Please stay." Her eyes reflect the desperation that she barely manages to keep out of her voice.

"Whatever you need, Lilah," I tell her, and I mean it. I will give her anything.

She starts to lift her shirt over her head and I turn and pull a fresh shirt for me. When I glance back at her, she's shucking off her jeans and my shirt falls mid-thigh. I breathe deep to keep my libido in check. Tonight is about making sure Lilah feels safe.

She pulls back the covers and climbs under. I flick off the light and slide in next to her. She grasps my arm and pulls my front to her back. I curl around her like armor, and that's where I finally fall asleep.

I wake to daylight thorough the window and the warm smell of vanilla all around me. When I open my eyes, Lilah is watching me. If she were anyone else, that would feel intensely creepy, but with her it sends a ripple of pleasure through my whole being. But as I scrub a hand over my face, wiping away the remnants of sleep, she sits up and tugs my baggy T-shirt off her pristine body. All I can do is stare as it hits the floor in a heap. She straddles me in just her panties and I resist the urge to reach for her and drag her to me. Her nipples are tight buds, so pink and perfect, and when she leans down and kisses me, the sizzle of her skin on mine lights my fire. I brush my fingertips over her back and goose bumps pebble her skin, making her shudder. She draws back and stares down at me with some expression that I can't quite name. All I do know is the ghosts that have been haunting her are gone from her eyes.

She rolls her hips, rubbing herself along the bulge in my jeans that there's no way I can stop.

She is so fucking perfect there aren't even words.

She flicks open the button of my jeans and drags down the fly, and when she lifts her hips and pulls her panties aside, I don't stop her. If this is what she needs from me right now, I'm not going to deny her. She wants to get lost, I can't imagine any safer place than in me. She sinks slowly down my hard cock and it's the most excruciating thing I've ever felt, pure pleasure so intense it's painful.

She keeps me mesmerized by the shining silver of her eyes, the feel of her body riding mine, the intensity of the electricity crackling between us. I grasp her thighs and start to move under her to her agonizingly slow rhythm, feeling her from the roots of my hair to the nails on my toes. She's everywhere inside me, leaving no room for the demons that have haunted me for so long. She starts pumping faster and I glide my thumb forward to her clit. Her head drops back and she vibrates with her moan as I press. While I work her clit with one hand, I trail my fingertips up her body and tease the pebbles of her nipple with my thumb. She arches into my hand, my palm cupping one perfect tit, and I've never wanted anything in my mouth as much as I want to taste that nub.

But this is her show. She's calling the shots. I let her take what she needs, knowing in the process she'll be giving me more than I could ever ask for. More than I deserve.

She fucks me, slow and steady, and her moans escalate to mewls, so base it's as if she devolves into pure need. Her movements become more frenetic as she gets closer to peaking and I begin to thrust harder into her. She rewards me by dropping her mouth open and crying out her release. I give her mine and come hard inside her.

She drapes her body over mine and moans her satisfaction softly into my ear.

This is fucking heaven.

Lilah stayed with me for three days. We didn't fuck again, but I listened while she sorted through everything. The last two days, she's been back with Destiny. They've been working things out between them and I've tried to stay out of the way, but it's Christmas and I have something for Lilah.

I've never been one to get all caught up in giving Christmas gifts, but I'm barely holding it together this morning because I want Lilah to have this. I'm up early and I hold off for as long as I can before shooting off a text. *I've got something for you. Can I come over?*

It's nine when she finally texts me back. *Okay. When?*

Now. I'm parked outside.

O_O

Sorry. I couldn't wait.

I shove open the door of the Torino and lift a hand to press the buzzer, but before I can, the door swings open and she's there. She's in one of my T-shirts and her hair is all over the place. There's nothing sexier on this entire planet than the way she looks when she just wakes up.

She tugs me inside and presses against me. "Merry Christmas."

"Merry Christmas," I say, drawing away and holding up a small box with a ribbon around it.

She takes it and looks a question at me.

"Just open it."

Instead, she takes my hand pulls me up the stairs. "I have something for you too."

When we get to the top, the family room is empty. We take seats on the couch and she pulls her guitar up from next to the arm. She rests it in her lap and starts strumming softly. "This still needs some work," she says, "but it's your Christmas present, so here goes."

And then she sings to my soul: a song about accepting what's happened and moving on; about forgiving; about learning to live again and allowing yourself to be happy.

When she's done, she sets the guitar aside and climbs astride my lap. "Thank you."

I shake my head. "I didn't do anything."

"You did. You've taught me that it's okay to live." She kisses me. "And to love."

"If I've given back anything for everything you've given me, then I'm happy, but I don't deserve any of the credit."

She smiles. "Shut up and kiss me."

I do as I'm told, because I'm helpless to resist her. When she finally draws away, I set her on the couch next to me and nod at her box. "Your turn."

She slips a finger gingerly under the ribbon.

"It's a gift," I say, "not an incendiary device."

She smiles and tugs harder, pulling the ribbon loose. When she opens the box, she just looks at the key to my apartment inside for a long moment before pinching it between her finger and thumb and pulling it out.

"I want you to know there's no part of my life that's not yours. Anytime you need somewhere to go, I want it to be my place you think of. I want it to feel like home to you."

She's still staring at the key. "I couldn't just walk in."

"Why not? I want you to."

"What if you're...I don't know, dancing around naked or whatever?"

I just look at her.

She shrugs. "Okay, I guess you're not a dancing around naked kind of guy, but you know what I mean."

"I don't."

She tosses a hand at me. "What if you're doing something private, or...with someone?"

My heart freezes. This isn't how I saw this going. I thought she'd get that me giving her a key is a huge deal, and it means I'm committed to her and this relationship. "That's really what you think of me?"

"I don't know what to think," she says, shoving a hand through her hair.

"You're joking, right?"

She shakes her head. "I've told you I love you at least half a dozen times. You've never said it back. I figured that meant you weren't ready for any sort of commitment."

I fix her in my gaze and pick the key I just had made yesterday out from between her fingers, holding it up for her to get a solid look at how new it is. "I've never done this before, Lilah. If you weren't sixteen, I'd be asking you to move in for real. I want you with me every second of every day. I will never be with anyone else because no one else is you. You're all I want…all I need." I press the key into her palm and close her fingers around it. "I want you to have this because I trust you and, even if I don't say it back, I love you."

"Well that's touching," Destiny says from the hall, and both Lilah's and my gaze snap to her. "Do you mean a word of it?"

I stand as she crosses past us to the kitchen. "Every single one of them."

Destiny glares at me as she pours a cup of coffee. "So my sister's not just your current flavor of the week?"

"There are no other fucking flavors," I say getting more than a little pissed. I almost open my mouth to tell her she was my last one of those and there hasn't been anyone but Lilah since, but rather than proving my point, that will only hurt them both.

"So you're saying you're going to stop bringing home barflies and college chicks from Sam Hill? Because old habits die hard, Bran." She glances at Lilah and back to me. "Does she have any clue how many women you've slept with?"

"Hundreds," Lilah says from behind me, and my stomach cramps at how slimy that makes me sound coming out of her mouth.

"Think about that number, Lilah," Destiny says, holding her sister in a hard gaze. "*Hundreds*. That's staggering. What makes you think you're not going to be just another number?"

"She's not just—" I start, but Lilah cuts me off.

"I'm not stupid, Destiny. I know Bran might break my heart. But if I have to choose between never taking the risk on something as intense as what I feel for Bran and nursing a hole in my chest, I'll take the hole every time."

Destiny shoots me a warning glare. "You took her to see our mother. Why would you do that?"

"Because she asked me to," I answer honestly. "There's nothing I wouldn't do for her if she asked."

"My mother nearly ruined us both. She's toxic. Lilah shouldn't be anywhere near her."

"I think that's Lilah's call."

Destiny's head shakes adamantly. "It's mine. I'm the one who looks out for her. I'm the one who protects her."

"I don't need protecting," Lilah says. "Especially from Bran."

"I don't like this, Lilah," Destiny warns.

"Are you going to report him to the cops?" Lilah asks.

"I should. This is wrong."

"But you won't."

Lilah can obviously read her sister, because Destiny blows out a breath. "Not unless he gives me a reason to."

Lilah takes my hand. "Even then. Promise me."

Destiny's jaw tightens when she glances at our interwoven fingers. "You're asking a lot, Lilah."

"Promise me," Lilah pushes.

Destiny spins on me. "She's only sixteen. She doesn't get how thoroughly a guy can ruin a girl. Do the right thing, Bran. Walk away."

"Destiny, stop!" She squeezes my fingers and tugs me closer. "I love Bran and this is happening."

Destiny drops into a kitchen chair and takes a long drink of coffee. "So, what now?"

Lilah shrugs. "It's Christmas. I guess we eat turkey."

"We can see if the PackMart has frozen dinners," Destiny says, tapping her nails on her mug.

I glance around their apartment. No tree. No gifts. And now, frozen dinners. "Come to Mom's with me."

They both look at me.

"It's just Brenda, me, and Mom and she's got this twenty pound turkey."

They look at each other, Lilah's face filled with hope and Destiny's with trepidation. At the same time, they nod. They may not be twins in the true sense, but they're sure as hell in each other's heads.

"When?" Lilah asks, turning to me.

"I'll be back for you at two?"

"We'll be ready." She takes my hand again and guides me to the door. We step through and I let her go first down the narrow stairs. She stops at the bottom and waits for me. "Thanks."

I tug her to me, pin her between me and the steel security door, and kiss the shit out of her. When we're both starving for air, I draw back and stare into her eyes. "I love you, Lilah. Don't fucking forget it."

She smiles up at me, holding up my key. "Got it, Sergeant Serious."

I open the door and head for the Torino, and it's hours before I can wipe this damn smile off my face.

CHAPTER 34

Lilah

The house smells like baking cookies and when I come out of my room dressed and ready, Destiny's putting plastic wrap over a plate mounded with little brown balls.

"Are you going to be good with this?" I ask, slipping on my boots. "We don't have to go if it's going to be weird for you."

She pulls back the cellophane and pushes the plate across the counter to me. "If you and Bran are a thing, I'm going to have to get used to being around him."

I pluck a cookie off the top of the stack. "I know how lame it sounds, but everything with us just clicked, you know? I mean...I know he's older and that should be a thing, but it's really not. I didn't mean for you to get hurt."

She pops a cookie into her mouth and chews. "I wasn't really hurt, Lilah. All I ever wanted to do was make sure you were safe and provided for. If you feel safe with Bran, then I'll try to be happy for you."

I take a bite of the cookie in my hand. It's like a little bit of heaven on my tongue. "Oh my god. What are these?"

"I improvised with what we had," she says with a shrug.

"You just made this up?" I ask, my mouth full of the rest of the cookie that I just crammed in.

"It's not hard," she says. "If you've got flour, sugar, baking powder, and butter, you can add a little of this and that and always come up with something that works."

I shake my head. "But not as good as this. You have a gift."

She smiles. "I got a job at Ambling Rose Bakery. Took some things I made over there and talked to the owner. I'm starting after New Year's."

I squeal a little and jump up, wrapping her in a hug. Not usually my thing, but this is so perfect for her. "This is so awesome. Everything is going to be amazing."

"She said Bran had already talked to her about me," she says against my shoulder. "He's been looking out for us, Lilah, and it's because he cares about you. I need to start trusting that you know what's right for you."

"You're not still mad that he took me to see Mom?" I ask.

"You needed answers. I get that."

"So, you won't be mad if I ask him to take me back?"

I've been thinking about how things happened that night. Mom nearly killed us in the fire, but I don't think she meant to. She was a shitty mother, but she took the brunt of Dad's temper so we didn't have to. And when push came to shove, she did what she had to do to save us.

She pulls away and looks at me. "You know what happened now. There's no reason to have to see her again."

"But I want to." I hold her gaze. "And I think you should come with me."

She starts shaking her head before the sentence is fully out of my mouth. "I can't."

"I didn't think I could either, but she's clean now, Destiny. She knows she let us down."

Her head is still shaking an adamant no. "I'm not giving her the satisfaction of feeling better about all the shit she did by letting her get it all off her chest. She needs to live with what she put us through."

"She is, Destiny. I don't think telling us she's sorry is going to clear her conscience."

The doorbell rings.

"That's our ride," she says, slipping on a sweater.

I pull on my jacket as she scoops the cookies up and we head down to meet Bran.

❖

Vicky's house is huge, nestled into thick evergreens at the base of a hill. When we pull up, I'm sure it has to be an inn or something.

"You've got to be fucking waxing me," Bran says as we wind to the top of the driveway. A gray Lincoln is parked near the three-car garage.

"What?" I ask.

He nods at the Town Car as we roll to a stop next to it. "Dad."

"That's a little weird," I say.

"Whatever," he says with a roll of his eyes.

We pile out of the car and Bran lays his hand on the small of my back, sending an electric thrill through my body. We follow as Destiny carries the plate of cookies up the long flagstone walk to the front door.

"Just walk in," Bran says when Destiny reaches for the doorbell.

She turns the knob and the smells of pine and cinnamon and turkey hit me in the face. Before we're even through the door, my mouth is watering.

"Destiny!" Vicky says, skirting around the island of a huge kitchen in an even more enormous great room that the door opens in to. "How have you been? I've been worried about you."

"I'm good," my sister says, stepping into Vicky's hug. She backs away and hands her the plate. "I know it's not much, but I made some cookies."

Vicky takes the plate and tugs the cellophane loose at one edge, taking a whiff. Her eyes widen and she plucks one out and takes a bite.

"Sweet Jesus in heaven," she says with a roll of her eyes. "Smith! You got to taste these."

A buff balding guy appears from a glass paneled doorway I can now see is a pantry. Bran has Vicky's eyes and mouth, but everything else is his father's.

Vicky holds out the plate and he tosses a whole cookie into his mouth. His eyes pop as he chews. "Holy shit."

"I need your recipe," Vicky says to Destiny.

Destiny cringes a little. "I didn't really write it down, but it's basically just a butter cookie with a little bit of nutmeg, clove and a drop of anise, because that's what I had."

"Christ, honey," Vicky says, swiping another. "You should open a cookie shop."

"Bran got me a job at Ambling Rose," Destiny says, giving him an appreciative nod.

Bran holds up his hands. "That wasn't me."

"Well, based on this," Vicky says, devouring the last bit of the cooking in her hand, "it's the smartest move Molly ever made."

Bran's dad snatches another cookie and Vicky slaps his hand. "I'm Smith Silo," he says, extending his free hand toward me. "Hear you're the girl who finally tamed my son."

I can't stop my eyes from widening. "Lilah." I take his hand. "And I didn't tame anything."

He gives me a firm shake and a wink. "If you say so, little girl."

I cringe, really not liking his nickname for me and hoping to God it doesn't stick.

"And you're Destiny," he says, shifting his hand to my sister.

"Nice to meet you, Smith," Destiny says, shaking his hand. Then she turns to Vicky. "What can we help with?"

They all head for the kitchen and Bran takes my hand and pulls me back when I start to follow. He yanks me to him and plants a firm, unyielding kiss to my mouth.

Everything inside me turns to warm mush at the way he just takes what he wants. But, as if he reads my mind, he always gives me what I need: a squeeze of my waist and a brush of his thumb over my cheek as he threads his fingers into my hair make me feel more needed and wanted than I ever have in my life. But before the rest of them turn around, he's let me go.

The door opens as we're passing and Brenda comes through with a guy in tow.

"Hey," Bran says. He tugs her into a quick, one-armed hug, then holds out his hand to the guy. "Good to see you again, Trevor."

"Bran," he says with a nod, shaking his hand.

Bran turns to me. "This is my girlfriend, Lilah,"

I can't explain the jolt of panic up my spine at the word, except that Bran using it makes me realize this is for real. We're really doing this.

"I don't know what you did to my brother," Brenda says as she swoops in for a hug, "but do more of it. I've never seen him so relaxed."

"Um…okay," I say.

"Brenda!" Vicky calls from the kitchen. "Get your butt over here and do whatever you do to these sweet potatoes to make them melt in my mouth."

"Coming, Ma," she calls and drags Trevor that way.

Bran and I follow.

"What you got for us, Ma?" Bran asks.

"If you can pick us something good out of the wine cellar, that would be great," she says.

Bran takes my hand and tows me to a door under the curved staircase that leads to the second floor. He opens it and flicks on a light, and we wind down a stone staircase into a damp, cool basement. We reach the bottom and I shiver at the temperature change.

"Cold?" he says, pulling me against his warm body.

I smile up at him. "Not anymore."

His smile is all sex as he leans down and kisses me. I kiss him back with everything I have, and before I know what's happened, my back is pressed again the stone wall and Bran's rock hard abs and pecs are crushed against the front of me. His kiss is ravenous and I let him devour me.

He lifts me and when I open my legs and wrap them around his waist, I feel every inch of him, hard and ready.

Maybe part of it is how over the line it would be to fuck Bran in his mother's wine cellar with everyone just upstairs, but I find myself reaching for the button of his jeans. "Will they come down here?"

By way of an answer, he slips a hand under my skirt and gives my nicest lace panties a sharp tug. They come away in shreds in his hand. I'm still struggling to get him out of his boxer briefs, so he does it for me. And when he sinks himself deep inside me, I moan so loudly that I'm sure everyone upstairs must have heard. I stop moving and listen, but there's Christmas music and chatter, and the banging of pots, pans and dishes in the kitchen.

When I look at Bran, he's giving me a devil's smile. "Merry Christmas."

He thrusts hard into me and forces a breathy "oh, God," up my throat.

"You're so fucking wet," he groans against my cheek.

"Because you make me so fucking horny," I gasp.

I hold onto his neck and leverage off the wall, moving with him and taking him as deep as I can. We move together and the cold of the basement turns to molten heat with our sex. I'm sweating under my sweater only minutes later. It doesn't last very long, but it's so intense that I have to bite into Bran's shoulder to keep from screaming when I come.

He gives me a few more sharp thrusts then comes deep inside me, tipping his head back and groaning, "Fuck, Lilah."

There's a long moment we just stay here, me pinned between the cold of the wall and the scorching heat of Bran's body, breathing hard. But then he kisses me and sets me down.

"Hope these weren't your favorites," he says, handing me my panties.

"They were, actually," I say.

Since I can't wear them, I use them to clean myself up, then Bran slips them into his pocket. "She'll want a red and a white," he says, walking over to shelves of racked wine near the stone wall in the back like what we just did happens every day.

I finger comb my hair back into place as he looks the rack over for a minute, then pulls one and reads the label. He puts it back and pulls the one next to it. Once he's decided on his choice, he hands it to me and goes to a refrigerator with a glass door at the end of the racks. He peers through the glass for a minute before opening the door and pulling a bottle.

He takes my hand and we head back upstairs. Bran sets the bottles on the counter and no one looks at us like anything's off. I shoot Bran a secret smile.

"Do the honors, Bran," his dad says, holding out an electric carving knife.

Bran walks to the other side of the island, where an immense turkey sits on a carving board, and goes to work. I watch him conquer the beast for a few minutes, then turn for the living room. The ceiling is vaulted, and Vicky has what must be a fifteen foot tree in front of the wall of windows that looks toward the mountains. It's all decked out in red and gold, with a golden star fixed to the top. There are ribbons and beads, shining glass globes and tinsel.

"I'll go," Destiny says from behind me. I turn and she's looking up at the star on top of the tree. She sighs and lowers her gaze to mine. "I hate Mom for what she did to us, and I'm not letting her off the hook, but if you want to go talk to her, I'll go with you."

I pull her into a hug. "Thank you."

"If it gets ugly, you won't be thanking me, Lilah. But I need answers too."

Her voice wavers on the last, and when I draw back, her eyes are moist. "Just listen to what she has to say, okay?"

She nods slowly. "I'll try."

"Oh my God!" Brenda says from the kitchen. We turn and find her holding half of one of Destiny's cookies. "What is this?" she asks Destiny, her eyes wide.

Destiny moves to the kitchen and I turn back to the tree. I skirt around the mound of gifts at the base and examine the decorations more closely. Some are clearly homemade by little hands. At eye level, right on the front of the tree, here's an ornament with painted red and green puzzle pieces glued into a wreath. And in the center is a picture of an adorable dark-haired little boy with a missing front tooth.

I lift it off the branch to get a closer look, and smile when Bran's strong hands slip around my waist from behind. He kisses my neck and I shudder.

"Thought I warmed you up downstairs," he mutters against my ear.

"You did," I say, shooting a look at the kitchen, where everyone is talking loudly over each other as they pull the meal together.

"C'mon," he says, taking my hand and tugging me toward the stairs. I think we might be going back downstairs for round two, but he leads me to the spiral stairs. "So, downstairs, this is pretty much it. The laundry room and bathroom are over there," he says, gesturing to a door between the kitchen and the living room. "And the bedrooms are all upstairs."

We pass a doorway at the top of the stairs. "Brenda's room," he says with a nod, pushing it open so I can see in.

It's not too different than I remember my room looking when my parents were still parents, double bed with a pink quilt and nondescript furniture.

He knocks on the next two doors as we pass. "Guest rooms." At the end of the hall, he pushes open a pair of double doors. "Mom's room."

It's huge, with a stone fireplace on one wall, antique furniture, and a king size bed on a chunky wooden frame.

He gives me a gentle nudge back toward the door across from the guest rooms. "My room."

It's austere with a plain navy comforter on a queen size bed and nothing on the walls, similar to his bedroom in his apartment. Except hanging on a corner of the mirror over the dresser are his dog tags.

I go over and lift them away from the mirror, sort of hating them. They're the source of his nightmares.

"Silo, B. S." I look up at him. "Smith, like your father?"

He nods, moving closer.

He slips the tags out my hand. "I hadn't slept in six years before I met you." He looks at them, rubbing them between his thumb and fingers. "I can't explain it, except to say when my life was meaningless, this was all there was to dream about. Now," he says, reaching for my face, "I've got something so much better."

He pulls me close and kisses me, then drops his tags on the dresser.

We kiss and I never want to stop, but Vicky's voice carries up the stairs. "Dinner's on!"

We head down to the dinner table and as we all sit and talk and eat way too much, I feel myself getting a little choked up. Destiny and Vicky are talking recipes, and Smith and Trevor offer to be their test subjects. Brenda asks me about my music and, as I tell her about the song I just wrote for her brother, I glance at Bran and find him smiling at me. It's not exactly Norman Rockwell, but it's more of a family than I've ever had. I don't even know half of these people at the table very well, but it feels warm and inviting and I've never felt so much like I belong.

And when Bran takes my hand under the table and squeezes, I know, as long as it lasts, this is where I want to be.

ACKNOWLEDGEMENTS

My most heartfelt thanks to my extremely patient husband, for providing basic life necessities and keeping us all sustained during my obsession with my imaginary friends. To my girls, for being a source of inspiration for everything that I do. To my parents who, from the beginning, taught me to believe in myself. To the incredible team at New Leaf, including but not limited to my omnipotent uberagent, Suzie Townsend, for being the most incredible advocate any author could have, and Danielle Barthel for everything she does behind the scenes. To Danielle Sanchez and the fabulous ladies at Inkslinger, who put up with me for some unknown reason. And my writer friends for all their incredible support.

And, because my Muse is a wannabe rock star, a special thanks to Sam Hunt for *Take Your Time*, the incredible song that brought Bran and Lilah to life in my head.

ABOUT THE AUTHOR

Mia Storm is a hopeless romantic who is always searching for her happy ending. Sometimes she's forced to make one up. When that happens, she's thrilled to be able to share those stories with her readers. She lives in California and spends much of her time in the sun with a book in one hand and a mug of black coffee in the other, or hiking the trails in Yosemite.

Connect with her online at MiaStormAuthor.blogspot.com, on Twitter at @MiaStormAuthor, and on Facebook at www.facebook.com/MiaStormAuthor.